THE GUNSMITH

444

Deadly Trouble

**Books by J.R. Roberts
(Robert J. Randisi)**

The Gunsmith series

Lady Gunsmith series

Angel Eyes series

Tracker series

Mountain Jack Pike series

COMING SOON!

The Gunsmith
445 – The Curse of the Gold City

For more information visit:
www.SpeakingVolumes.us

THE GUNSMITH

444

Deadly Trouble

J.R. Roberts

SPEAKING VOLUMES, LLC
NAPLES, FLORIDA
2019

ISBN 978-1-62815-988-2

Chapter One

The fall came out of nowhere.

Eclipse was surefooted, never stumbled or fell, but in this case it wasn't the Darley's fault, or Clint's. He couldn't have known that the earth at the top of the hill would give way like it did. But all of a sudden both Clint and the horse were hurtling down the hill in free fall. He heard the horse's squeals of frustration as they tumbled, yelled out his own displeasure as he banged his knees, elbows and keister on jagged rocks all the way down.

Finally, he rolled as they hit bottom and came to rest. For the first moment Clint remained lying there on his back, testing his limbs to see if any of them were broken. They seemed to move and flex, although painfully. Finally, he pushed himself into a seated position, trying his limbs again, waiting for his head to clear. His hat had flown off, was lying off somewhere. He used his hands to probe his head for possible wounds, and came away with blood on his left palm. Next, he checked for his gun, found that it had fallen out of the holster.

That was when he heard Eclipse.

The horse's whinnies and snort, sounded as if he was in distress.

"Damn it!" Clint said, pushing himself to his feet. He looked around, saw that Eclipse was about six feet from where he was standing, lying on his side. "Oh, no!"

He ran to the Darley and knelt down next to him.

"Easy, boy, easy," he said, putting his hands on the animal's neck to try to keep him calm. At that point the horse tried to stand, but he squealed in pain while doing so. It was only Clint using his weight that kept Eclipse from forcing himself to his feet, possibly doing more damage.

"Easy," he said, again stroking the big horse's neck. "Take it easy. Just lie still and let me check you over."

The saddle had come askew, so Clint took the time to remove it and toss it aside.

"There you go," he said to Eclipse. "Now just lie still."

He started running his hands over the horse's flanks and withers, up and down his legs. On the right side, at the base of the neck, it looked as if a large, sharp stone had taken a piece out of the flesh. It was bleeding pretty badly, starting to pool beneath Eclipse.

"Damn!" Clint swore, again. He went to the discarded saddle, dug into his saddlebags and came out with a shirt. Going back to his fallen companion, he balled the shirt up and tried to stop the flow of blood.

Further examination showed that one of Eclipse's legs was damaged. The Darley couldn't straighten it, and if he had tried to stand, he certainly would have done more damage. Clint just hoped it wasn't broken.

While he was trying to decide what to do next, the blood from his own scalp wound started to seep into his eyes, and his left leg hurt. He looked down and saw, like the horse, that his leg had been punctured by something during the fall.

"Looks like we're both pretty banged up, big fella," he said. "You're going to need a vet, and I'm going to need a sawbones. Only thing is, where are we going to find them out here?"

He looked around, but there was nothing to see but rocks and trees. It was all the great plains of Montana had to offer, at the moment.

Clint steadied Eclipse, convinced the animal to lie still, then got to his feet to look around. He knew they were west of Billings, but it was far off. He was going to need a town closer by.

He looked up to the top of the hill they had tumbled down. There hadn't been time to look around before the loose earth had given way beneath them. He was going to have to take himself back up the steep slope on foot, to see what he could.

However, when he took a step his left leg buckled beneath him, and he found himself seated on the ground next to the Darley Arabian.

"We're really in a mess this time, fella," he said. "I'm going to need help getting back up this hill, and you'll just have to keep lying still."

The horse stared at him, then rolled his eyes. There was a white lather beginning to build on him, probably from more than just the heat. The horse might have been in a state of shock.

"Okay," Clint said, touching the horse's neck gently, "I'm going to have to try this again."

He looked down at his left leg. The pants were soaked with blood, and some of it had seeped into his boot. Before long, it would start pooling in his boot, soaking his sock. It would be hard to walk anywhere, that way.

"I'm going to need something to lean on, to help me climb," he said, more to himself than to the horse. "Like a nice thick branch."

He got back to his feet, careful not to put too much weight on his left leg until he found something he could use as a walking stick.

He took a few tentative steps, then a few more, until he was sure he could stand. Then he started a search of the immediate area for a likely stick.

Twenty feet from where Eclipse continued to lie, Clint found a fallen tree branch that seemed sturdy enough for his purpose. He leaned on the branch and walked back to the fallen horse.

"I'm going to try to go up the hill now. Just lie still and wait."

He hoped that the distress the animal felt would not eventually cause him to try and rise. Blood was seeping through the wadded up shirt, and he was obviously still unable to bend his injured leg.

Hopefully, from the top of the hill Clint would be able to see a town, or perhaps a house.

He took his first step to try and ascend the slope when he saw something at the top that stopped him.

An Indian, staring down at him.

Chapter Two

Clint waited to see what the Indian was going to do. After a few moments, the man withdrew. Clint decided to wait several moments more before taking the climb up the slope. Before long he saw the Indian come around from the other side. He had found another way down, rather than use the steep slope.

And he was alone.

As the man approached, Clint saw that he was very old, with a face full of wrinkles and long gray hair touching his shoulders.

"You are injured," the brave said.

"Yes," Clint said, "but my horse is hurt badly. We fell from the top of this hill."

The old brave walked over to where Eclipse was lying.

"I see," he said.

"Are you alone?" Clint asked.

"Oh, yes," the brave said. "I am useless to my people at my age. So I travel alone."

"What tribe are you from?"

"I am Salish."

Clint had heard of the Bitterroot Salish tribe, but had never met one of their people.

"Your horse needs help," the Salish said.

"I know. I was going to climb back up to the top to see if I could spot a town, or a house."

"There is no house or town near here," the Salish said. "I was once a medicine man. I will do what I can for you and your horse."

"We'd both appreciate that," Clint said. "But I think I'm going to have to find a vet for him. Do you have a horse somewhere?"

"I am on foot."

"I'll have to walk, then," Clint said.

"Can you?"

Clint tested his left leg again.

"I'll have to try."

The Salish looked at Clint's leg, and head.

"Let me treat your wounds," the Salish said, "and then I will treat your horse."

"Treat us with what?"

"I have a medicine bag on the other side of the hill. I will return."

"Thank you."

The old man moved quickly back around the hill, while Clint leaned over Eclipse. When he returned he was carrying a leather bag.

"Sit here," he said to Clint. "I will tend to you."

Clint came over and sat on a rock.

"What's your name?" Clint asked.

"You can call me Ben."

"Ben?" Clint asked. "Is that a Salish name?"

"No," the man said. "The Salish cast me out, so I took a white man's name."

"Just Ben?" Clint asked.

The man nodded. "Just Ben."

Ben cleaned Clint's head wound, then had him lower his trousers rather than rip them in order to treat the leg wound. He cleaned and bandaged it, using Clint's only other shirt as a cloth.

"Thank you," Clint said, "but now my horse."

They both went to Eclipse, and Clint had to calm him, talk to him, before the animal allowed the Salish, Ben, to lay his hands on him.

"He is hot with fever," Ben said. "I will clean his wound."

Ben removed the bloody shirt, cleaned Eclipse's wound, then took off his own shirt and used it to clot the gash on the animal's neck.

Next he addressed the leg.

"I am sorry," Ben said, "but I think it is broken."

"How badly?"

Ben felt the leg again, while Clint held Eclipse down so he wouldn't buck.

"It is probably fractured. If he tries to stand, he will snap it."

"He needs a vet."

"Even a white medicine man might not help him, but yes, that would be wise."

"I'm going to have to start walking to find one," Clint said. "Can you give me some idea of what direction to take?"

"Continue east," Ben suggested. "You should come to something—a house, a settlement—before you reach Billings."

Clint had been so concerned about Eclipse that this was the first time he looked around for his gun He found it lying in the dirt nearby, and knew he was going to have to clean it.

"But it will be dark soon," Ben said. "Better to build a fire and rest. You can get started in the morning, when you are stronger."

"But what about Eclipse's fever?"

"There is a water hole nearby," Ben said. "I will use the water to try to keep his fever down."

Clint gave it some thought and said, "All right, you're probably right about getting some rest. I have food and coffee in my saddlebag that I can share with you."

"I am grateful," Ben said. "You build the fire and I will go for the water. We will do what we can for this magnificent animal."

Chapter Three

They took turns bathing Eclipse with water, which grew cooler as the night progressed. Ben especially enjoyed the coffee and bacon Clint prepared, so Clint let him have most of it.

One of them sat up with the Darley all night, and it was Clint who took the last shift so that he was there when the sun came up.

He made a fresh pot of coffee and then woke Ben, who immediately came awake. In the morning light, the old Indian looked to be 70 or 80 years old, but he got to his feet swiftly and went to check on Eclipse.

"He still has fever, but not high," he said. "And the leg is swollen."

"Then I better get started," Clint said.

"How is your leg?"

Clint flexed it. It felt stiff and sore, but held his weight.

"I probably don't need a walking stick, but I'll take it anyway, just in case."

Ben went and got the thick branch. Apparently, during the night, he had done some work with his knife. It was almost completely smoothed out. It now looked like something you would find in an Indian tipi.

"Walk with it in both hands," he told Clint handing it to him. "It will be more helpful that way."

"I'll remember."

Clint went over to Eclipse and leaned to stroke his neck.

"You take it easy, partner," he said. "I'll be back with help."

He looked at the clear sky, grateful for it. If it rained, that wouldn't help the horse at all. He wished he had a tent to erect over him.

"Go!" Ben said. "The quicker you go, the quicker you will return."

"Right."

Clint left Ben all the food and coffee. He offered to leave the canteen, but the Indian said, "I have the water hole. You take the canteen."

That made sense. Clint had a feeling he still wasn't thinking straight after the bump on his head.

So with his gun and canteen he set out. He left the rifle behind, because all Ben had was his knife, and Clint couldn't carry the rifle and the walking stick.

He set off, heading east.

***

12

His leg began to act up almost immediately, and he took to leaning on the walking stick more than he thought he would. However, while he did not come to any houses or settlements in the first two hours, the stiffness in his leg began to ease the more he walked. There was still some pain when he put his weight on it, but it wasn't as stiff as when he started out.

After several hours of walking—or limping—he paused to take a short rest. A glance at the sky told him it was not yet noon. There was still plenty of the day left.

He drank some water, shook the canteen to discover it was less than half full. He needed to come across a well or a water hole.

He started walking again, studying the ground in the hopes of finding some tracks he might follow to civilization. It would even have been helpful to cross paths with a stage or carriage somewhere along the way, to get a lift to a town. But there was not even a dust cloud anywhere ahead of him. Just desolation.

Past noon he started to run out of water. He would have to save the dregs so as not to go completely dry.

It had to be nearly three when his legs began to give out—particularly the injured one. He leaned even more heavily on the walking stick, so much so that it snapped in half as dusk began to fall.

And then so did he . . .

Chapter Four

When he woke there was a ceiling over his head.

He frowned, stared at the many cracks there. He tried to remember what had happened. He could recall the tumble down the hill, both he and Eclipse being injured. He remembered some help . . . Ben, the Salish Indian. But . . . how had he come to be here?

Then he remembered the smooth walking stick, the long trek on foot, the stick snapping and then . . . nothing.

Warily, he sat up, found that he was on a bed. Not in it, beneath the covers, but lying atop the bed clothes, still dressed—except that his boots had been removed, and the leg of his trousers cut. He reached down, found that his leg had been freshly bandaged. He felt his head. No bandage there, but no blood, either.

Next, he looked around, saw that he was in a small room, with a chest of drawers that had seen better days, tattered curtains on the single window, through which no light came. It was night.

He swung around, brought sock-covered feet to the floor. It was bare wood, much trod upon from the looks of it. As he tried to stand he got dizzy, sat back down. Slowly, he thought, slowly.

Somebody had obviously found him lying unconscious, brought him here and tended to his wounds. He
had to assume there were only good intentions in this—
and then he slapped his thigh as he felt for his gun. It
wasn't there.

He searched the room, but didn't see the gun belt
hanging, anywhere.

Uncomfortable now, he again tried standing, this time
with success. He looked more carefully for the gun, but it
was nowhere in sight. But there was a closet, and a chest
of drawers, so he had to check both. That meant walking.

He tested his left leg, found that it held his weight,
though it still felt stiff. He took a step, then another. The
chest of drawers was closest to him, so he walked there
and leaned on it. It was flimsy, however, so he did not put
his full weight on it.

He took a moment or two, then started to open the
drawers. He didn't need to go any further than the top
one, which is where he found his gun and holster, neatly
coiled. He retrieved them. After strapping on the holster
he immediately felt better.

The door to the room opened and a woman stepped in.
She was middle-aged, angular, with long dark hair that
was shot with grey. Her dress was old and tattered, but
clean.

"Ya won't be needin' that," she assured him, "but if it makes ya feel better, ya might as well keep it on."

"Thank you for your kindness," he said. "I assume you're responsible for . . . this." He indicated his freshly wrapped leg.

"I found ya lyin' out there and brought ya here," she said. "I couldn't very well leave you to die, could I?"

"I'm happy you felt that way."

"Ya want help gettin' back to the bed?"

"Please."

She walked to him and he leaned on her. She was strong, took all of his weight, and walked him to the bed. There was nothing overtly sexual about the situation, yet he felt his body react to hers, which was obviously bare beneath the dress.

She helped him sit on the bed and then backed away, then stood with her hands on her hips and studied him.

"You look better," she said.

"Better than when?" he asked. "How long have I been here?"

"Only since yesterday."

"It's dark out. This is the second night I'm here?"

"Yes."

"Damn it!"

"It's not so bad. Like I said, you're lookin' better. You wanna eat somethin'?"

"What's your name?"

"I go by Zelda," she said. "Zelda Carter."

"Zelda, I've got to get back to my horse," he said. "We both fell, and he got hurt worse than I did. Is there a vet nearby?"

"Not nearby, no," she said. "The nearest town is about twenty miles."

"Damn it!" he swore, again. That was a long walk.

"How bad hurt is he?"

"He was bleeding, but we got that stopped. He's also got a leg that swelled up, and maybe broke, and a fever."

"Well," she said, "I treat all my own animals. I could have a look."

"Are you a vet?"

"Not really," she said. "I just got lots of animals, including a horse, that I take care of."

Clint took a moment to think.

"Look," she said, "why don't you let me give you somethin' to eat? Then you get some sleep and decide what you wanna do in the mornin'."

"Twenty miles, you said?"

"That's right."

He didn't really have any idea how far he had come, but it sure hadn't been twenty miles. They were closer to Eclipse than they were to the next town. If he waited til he got to that town to find a vet, who knew when they would get back to the injured horse?

"You have horses?" he asked.

"One," she said, "and a buckboard."

They could get back to Eclipse much quicker on a buckboard, and if she knew what she was doing, she could help him.

So far, she seemed to know what she was doing in treating him.

"Whataya say?" she asked. "Are ya hungry?"

He hadn't noticed it til now, but he was starved, and he could smell the food.

"Yeah, I am."

"Then let's eat," she said. "You can come to the kitchen, wash up, and I'll feed ya."

Chapter Five

Clint washed up in the kitchen sink while Zelda ladled out two bowls of beef stew from her stove. By the time he got to the kitchen table, his bowl was waiting for him. He picked up his spoon and took a big taste.

"Wow," he said, "this is mighty good."

"I'm glad you think so," she said. "All you was able to keep down yesterday was some soup."

"Really? I don't remember any of that."

"I don't wonder," she said. "You was really out of it."

"Well, I'm tasting it now," he said, grabbing a hunk of warm bread. "I hope you're as good treating animals as you are cooking them."

"I got some whiskey around here somewhere," she said. "You wanna try some?"

"Sure," Clint said, "I'm hungry enough to try anything."

She found a bottle of whiskey, brought it to the table with two glasses, and they proceeded to eat and drink.

He found out she had been living there alone for years, since her husband had died. Every so often she hitched up the horse and drove her buckboard to that town twenty miles away, for supplies.

"What town is it?" he asked.

"It's called Halsey," she said, "and it ain't really much of a town. It's got a general store, and a blacksmith, and I kin usually use both."

"And a vet?"

"There was one last time," she said. "If we kin get your horse back here, then I kin go and get 'im for ya."

"Let's see what you can do for him tomorrow," Clint said. "I don't know if he'll be able to walk this far."

"Well," she said, "if we got to, we kin stay out there with him til he's ready. I got a tent we can put over him."

"That sounds great," Clint said.

"How long you had that horse?"

"A lot of years," he said. "We've been through a lot together."

"I kin tell ya think a lot of 'im," she said. "The way you call 'im a him and not it."

"He's definitely a him," Clint said. "He's smart and has his own personality."

"What's his name?"

"Eclipse."

"What the hell is an eclipse?"

"It's when the sun is covered over by the moon," Clint said. "Happens every so often."

Her eyes brightened.

"I think I seen me one of them!"

"You probably have, living out here all this time."

From across the table he could see she was in her late thirties, although he had first thought forties. She must have been working hard for a long time, and it showed on her face and in her eyes. Her hands and arms were strong, though, and he knew her legs were too, the way she had supported his weight. Also, she had gotten him from where she found him all the way here to her house, inside and onto her bed and that took a lot of strength.

By the time they finished eating, the bottle of whiskey was empty. It hadn't been full to start with, but there had been enough that they were both feeling the effects.

She helped him from the kitchen back to the bedroom, and they both staggered a bit along the way. When she got him onto the bed, she sat down next to him.

"Where have you slept the two nights I've been in your bed?" he asked.

"On the floor in the kitchen," she said. "Made myself comfortable with some blankets."

"I hate taking your bed away from you, Zelda," he said. "Also, I wish there was some way I could thank you for what you've done."

"Well," she said, "I may be sayin' this because I'm some drunk, but I think there may be a way ya kin."

"How's that?"

"You could lemme sleep in the bed with ya," she said. "I know I said I was comfortable on the floor, but it ain't like bein' in a bed." She patted the mattress. "And it's big enough for the both of us."

"Sure it is," he said, moving over. "Yeah, sure, when you're ready to go to sleep, come ahead."

"Well, seein' as how I get up so early to start work," she said, "and I'm some drunk, like I said, I'd jest as soon go to bed now."

"I'm kind of tired myself," he said.

"And you ain't been under the sheets yet, so if ya wanna, git yourself under there."

She stood up, and he got up on the other side and pulled the sheet down. He wondered if he should keep his clothes on, but they were dirty from all the rolling in the dirt he had done, so he decided to remove his shirt and trousers. He pulled his pants off, then unbuttoned his shirt, tossed it away and got under the covers.

When he did, he saw that she had been watching him undress. Now, while he watched her, she grabbed the dress at the button and pulled it up over her head. Like he had thought, she was naked underneath.

She had some sharp angles to her body, like he had noticed the first time, but now that she was naked he saw she also had some curves. Her breasts weren't big, but they had solid undersides and light colored nipples. Her hip bones were kind of sharp, but she had long, muscular legs, enjoyed the way her skin felt against his.

She pulled the sheet back and got into bed with him. He could feel the heat coming off of her.

"You know," she said, "it's been some time since I been in bed with a man."

"Zelda—"

"So that's another way you might wanna thank me for what I done," she said. She reached down, stuck her hand inside his underwear and took a hold of his already hard cock. "You mind if I take these here skivvies off'a ya?"

The way her hand felt on him, he wasn't about to argue with her.

"Zelda," he replied, "I've got to say I don't much mind at all."

Chapter Six

Zelda may not have had a man in her bed for a long time, but she knew what to do when she got one.

Her body was powerful, her hands assured in their touches. The room was lit by a small lamp, leaving them mostly in shadows. Beneath the covers, she grasped his penis and stroked it, while kissing his chest. She kissed her way down until she was able to replace her hands with her mouth and tongue, licking the length of his hard cock. At the same time, she was careful of his injured leg.

For a woman who said she hadn't had sex in a long time, and who lived alone in the middle of nowhere, he wondered where she had learned what she was doing to him at that moment.

She took his long, hard cock into her mouth and sucked it wetly, moaning the whole time. She kept it up until he thought his penis would burst, and then she released him and crawled up on top of him.

Pressing her body tightly against his, trapping his cock between them, she kissed him, again, avidly, like a thirsty woman who had finally made it to water. He could hardly breathe, but made no attempt to dislodge her or push her away. Instead, he ran his hands down her back until he had both her butt cheeks clasped. Holding her that way, he rubbed her bushy pubic patch over his erection, then finally poked his way through it to slide inside of her.

She was wet and waiting, and when he pierced her, she moaned into his mouth and, without breaking the kiss, began to bounce her hips up and down, riding him.

Then, abruptly, she broke the kiss and sat up, continuing to bounce. He reached up and took hold of her breasts, which were firm enough not to bounce very much. The nipples dug into his palms. Hard work had certainly toned her body, as there was not an ounce of fat on her.

She began to grunt as her time approached, pressing her hands down on his belly so she could bounce even harder. He just hoped he could hold out long enough for her. He did, but not by much, for as she screamed and went into spasms of delight and pleasure, he also yelled, exploding inside of her . . .

***

They laid together a few moments after, and then she rolled onto her back.

"I needed that," she said. "You don't know how I needed that."

"And is that why you rescued me and brought me back here?" he asked, teasing.

"I didn't think of it, then," she said. "Only when I got you here . . . in my bed."

"And while I was unconscious?"

She looked at him, her eyes wide, and blurted, "I never did anythin'—I didn't touch—oh, you're teasin' me."

He laughed, then winced as he moved his left leg.

"Did I hurt you?" she asked, worried.

"No, not at all," he said. "You were very . . . careful. For a woman who hasn't had sex in so long, you sure were . . . good."

"My husband and me, we had sex all the time," she said. "We tried all kinds of things."

"A lot of men—a lot of married couples—like it only one way," he commented.

"Well," she said, "we didn't have much else to do but work and have sex, so we made the most of both."

"Your place looks like its fallen on hard times," he said.

"Yeah, since he died, I ain't been able to keep it up."

"Maybe I can help, then," he said. "I mean, because you helped me—"

"You paid me back a lot already," she said.

"No, I meant money," he said.

"I ain't no whore!" she snapped.

"I didn't mean that at all," he hurried to say. "I just meant I wanted to help."

She reached down to his crotch and grasped his semi-hard cock.

"Oh, yeah," she said, "I can see you wanna help me some more."

She rolled over on top of him, still mindful of his leg.

Chapter Seven

Clint woke in the morning with Zelda lying on his left arm. Normally he wouldn't have minded, since his gun hand was free, but the arm was numb, so he slid it out from beneath her without waking her.

He got out of bed, walked into the main part of the house, which combined the living room and kitchen. He looked out the window, saw a corral and barn that were in much need of repair. If they got back here with Eclipse, he decided he would stay a bit, do some repairs, if Zelda wasn't going to take any money from him.

They'd had sex two more times before falling asleep. She must have been exhausted and he hated to wake her, but he did need to get back to Eclipse as soon as possible.

He decided to make use of the pot-belly stove and have coffee ready for her when she got up. He was drinking his first cup when he heard horses outside. He looked out the window, saw three riders approaching. He went back into the bedroom long enough to fetch his trousers and gun belt, still without waking Zelda.

He quickly pulled on the pants, and slid his gun from the holster, which he left on the kitchen table. By then the men had reached the house, dismounted, and were knocking on the door.

"Come on, Zelda!" one of them shouted. "We told you we'd be here this mornin'!"

Clint went to the door and opened it, keeping his gun hand hidden.

"Can I help you?"

All three men stared at him in surprise. One was in his fifties, the other two their twenties. The resemblance told him they were father and sons.

"Who the hell are you?" the older man asked.

"I was about to ask you the same question," Clint said. "I'm a guest, you fellas are intruders. So . . . who are you?"

"My name's Kent Wheeler," he said, "These are my boys, Dave and Leonard."

"What do you want?" Clint asked.

"I wanna talk to Zelda," Wheeler said.

"She's asleep," Clint said. "When she wakes up I'll tell her you were here."

"No," Wheeler said, "I wanna talk to her now!"

"Sorry," Clint said. "I'm not going to wake her."

"Pa," Dave said, "you want us to—"

Both boys were carrying rifles, so Clint brought his hand out from behind the door so they could see the gun.

"Shut up!" Wheeler told his son. He pointed a finger at Clint. "You tell 'er I was here."

"I will."

"And I'll see you again."

"I'm sure you will," Clint said.

He stood and watched while the three men walked to their horses, mounted up and rode off. When he closed the door, he saw Zelda standing in the doorway to the bedroom, wearing a robe.

"What was that all about?" he asked her.

She sniffed the air.

"You made coffee," she said, ignoring his question.

"I did. You want a cup?"

"Oh God, yes."

"Have a seat, Ma'am."

She sat at the table while he poured her a cup and brought it to her.

"Lemme drink this, then I'll make some breakfast and we can go get your horse."

"Well," he said, "have a look at him, anyway."

"Yeah."

He sat across from her.

"What did Mr. Wheeler want?"

"He introduced himself?"

"And his sons, Dave and Leonard," Clint said. "When I say it like that, they sound like dogs."

"They are," she said. "Animals, I mean. All three of them."

"And who are they?" Clint asked. "I mean, to you."

"Neighbors."

"I thought you lived in the middle of nowhere."

"The Wheeler place is about thirty miles away," she told him.

"What could he want with you that brings him pounding on your door this early?"

"He wants to buy my place."

"Oh? As run down as it is?" he asked.

"He thinks he can make somethin' of it."

"And can he?"

"I don't know," she said, "but I ain't sellin'. It's all I got."

"Do you think you can bring it back?" Clint asked. "I mean, what was your husband's business?"

"Horses," she said. "That's why I think maybe I can help yours."

"Well, we'll find out," he said.

"I'll make some eggs," she said, standing, "and then we'll go."

"Suits me," he said. "I'll get dressed."

Chapter Eight

After a quick breakfast Zelda dressed in a shirt and trousers, while Clint went out and hitched the horse to the buckboard.

"This boy's kind of old," he said, as they climbed up.

"He's twelve," she said. "I raised him from a colt."

"Would you like me to drive?" he asked.

"No, I'll take the reins," she said. "Ol' Toby can be hard to handle sometimes."

"Whatever you say."

As they went along Clint asked, "How desperate is Wheeler to buy your place? I mean, he came with his sons, who had rifles."

"They probably wanted to scare me into sellin'," she said.

"Could they?"

"Not a chance," she said. "Take more than Kent Wheeler and his two boys to scare me into doin' anythin'."

"They'll probably come back," he warned.

"Again and again, I guess," she said. "They'll keep tryin' until one of us gets tired."

"Have they used force yet?"

"No," she said.

"From what I saw today, they will," Clint said. "So there may still be another way I can repay you."

"We'll see," she said.

***

Clint was surprised to see how far he had walked, but finally they came over a rise and saw the Salish, Ben, sitting with Eclipse, who didn't seem to have moved.

"You are back," Ben said, unnecessarily.

"Yes," Clint said, getting down from the buckboard. "This is Zelda."

"She is a medicine woman?" he asked.

"Kinda," Zelda said.

"Zelda, this is Ben."

"Bitterroot Salish, right?" she asked.

"That is correct."

She crouched down next to Eclipse.

"What've you done for him?" she asked.

"Tried to keep the fever down," Ben said. He looked at Clint. "Did you bring food?"

"We did, back of the buckboard. Help yourself."

Ben went to do that while Zelda looked Eclipse over.

"This is a fascinating animal," she commented. "I don't think I've ever seen one like him, before. Arabian?"

"Yes," Clint said. "How is he?"

33

He waited a few more moments until she completed her examination.

"The wound isn't bleeding, but it's infected," she said. "I'll have to clean it thoroughly. You're gonna have to make sure he lays still."

"I'm surprised he's doing that now, and letting you touch him," Clint said.

"He's sick and he knows it. He also knows I can help him."

"What about his leg?"

"I don't think it's broken, but there must be some broken blood vessels in there. It's swollen, also infected. I'm gonna have to drain it."

"Can you treat both at the same time?"

"I'll clean the open wound," she said. "After that, I'll be able to deal with the leg. Then we'll have to watch both wounds."

"Can he get up?"

"He might be able to," she said, "but he can't walk back to my place, yet. I'll have to erect the tent."

"Wait a minute," Clint said. "What if we can get him on the buckboard?"

"How?"

"You said he can stand," Clint said. "He can walk to the buckboard."

"And how do we get him on it?"

34

"He might be able to do that himself," Clint said. "If not, maybe we can build a ramp. Then he can walk on and lie down."

"And we'll be able to get him back to my place to watch him," she said.

"Can't we take him back there for you to treat him?"

"I'll want to treat him before we let him stand up," she said. "So we'll need a fire."

"I will build one," Ben said, returning with bacon grease on his face.

"Good," she said. "I brought some tools I can use to clean and cauterize the wound, then do the same thing to his leg, once I drain it."

"So we'll be here a while, anyway," Clint said.

"Yes."

"And the tent?"

She looked up at the sky.

"It doesn't look like the weather's gonna turn," she said. "If it does, we can get the tent up quick."

"Okay," Clint said, "then I guess we better get started."

Chapter Nine

They built a fire so Zelda could cauterize Eclipse's wound. At the same time, they made coffee and fried some more bacon for Ben.

Clint remained by Eclipse's side while Zelda worked on the open wound. She removed the wadded up shirt/bandage, cleaned the wound out, and cauterized it with a hot branding iron while Clint held Eclipse down and still, as best he could.

Before starting on the horse's leg Zelda paused for a cup of coffee. She took a flask from her pocket and spiked it with whiskey, which Clint refused, but Ben accepted.

"Your horse is a good patient," she said to Clint.

"He's smart enough to lie still and let you treat him," Clint said. "But I know he's in pain."

"Most of his pain is from the leg," she said. "I'll take care of that next. Once I drain it, it won't hurt as much."

"Then let's get to it."

They put down their empty cups and went back to where Eclipse was lying still. The horse's eyes followed Clint as he once again sat down on the ground next to him.

"Easy, boy," he said, stroking the animal's neck. "I know you're in pain, but we're going to fix it."

Once again, Zelda used the fire to heat the tools she needed to cut Eclipse's leg open and drain out the infection. Once that was done, she cauterized and bandaged it. By this time it was getting dark.

Once again they had coffee, supped on bacon and beans from Zelda's stores.

"You did a good job keeping his fever down," she said to Ben. "You probably kept him alive."

"I did what I could."

"Tomorrow Clint wants to try and get Eclipse onto the buckboard."

"I will help," Ben said.

He was old, and thin, weighed 120 pounds if he was lucky, but he was strong enough and smart enough to be of assistance to them.

"Good," Zelda said. "we'll try and get him up on his feet in the morning."

"Let's set a watch," Clint said. "Three hours each."

"Are you expectin' trouble?" Zelda asked.

"Always," Clint said.

"Well," she said, "I'll sleep next to your horse, just in case."

"That sounds like a good idea."

***

The weather remained mild during the night, so there was still no point in erecting the tent for shelter.

Zelda woke the next morning, rolled over and immediately checked on Eclipse.

"How is he?" Clint asked, walking over with two cups of coffee.

"His fever's down," she said, accepting one. "That's from cleaning out the infections."

"Good," Clint said. "Let's have some breakfast and then we'll try to get him up on his feet."

She nodded. They went to the fire, made some bacon-and-eggs, which Ben enjoyed immensely. Zelda even used a second pan to make some corn bread.

"That was the finest meal I have had in a long time," the Indian said to her. "Thank you."

"If you want," she said, "you can come with us to my place and stay a while. You can help with some work, and I'll give you even better meals than this one."

"That sounds good," he said. "I will come."

"Good," Clint said, "now that it's settled, let's see about getting Eclipse to your place."

The three of them got up and walked to where the Darley Arabian was lying.

"Okay, boy," Zelda said, putting her hands on him, "let's see if you can get up onto your feet."

He laid quiet for a moment, then lifted his head. He set it down, then lifted it again and made an effort to rise. They stood back to give him room. This time he lifted his head up, got one foreleg under hip, protecting the injured one, and struggled to his feet, doing most of the work with his back legs.

And then he was up.

"That was great, boy!" Clint praised, stroking his neck.

"Real good," Zelda said, "but we still got a long way to go."

"Come on, fella," Clint said, "let's take a walk."

He walked the horse around a bit, the Darley limping on one front leg. Finally, Clint walked him over to the buckboard and stopped at the back.

"Under normal circumstances he'd be able to jump up there easily," Clint said.

"Let's give him some time to get used to the idea," Zelda said. "If he can't do it himself, we'll have to find some way to make a ramp."

But they were shocked when Eclipse simply jumped up onto the buckboard, and stood there.

"Mission accomplished," Clint said.

Chapter Ten

When they managed to get Eclipse to lie down in the back of the buckboard, Ben retrieved his horse, and followed Zelda and Clint back to her place.

Along the way, Clint saw three riders who seemed to be pacing them, riding along with them, but at a distance. At first he thought it might be more Salish Indians, but he was eventually able to tell that they weren't Indians, they were white men. And the only white men he knew of who were interested in Zelda were the Wheelers. He decided not to say anything to Zelda, so she wouldn't worry.

One look exchanged with Ben, however, revealed that he, too, had spotted the riders.

When they reached the ranch she stopped the buckboard in front of the barn.

"We can bed him down in here," she said. "That is, if we can get him down from the buckboard without doing any more harm. His hind legs got him up, but he's going to have to come down on his front legs."

"Now that we're here," Clint said, "and not out in the middle of nowhere, I'm sure we can fashion a ramp so he can just walk down."

"Of course," she said.

"I'll bet Ben and I can find the makings in the barn," he said.

"Okay, do that," she said. "I'll go inside and prepare a meal for when you're done."

"That sounds good," Ben said.

She smiled at the old Salish.

"You'll see," she said. "I'll make you a meal like you've never had before."

"Ben, why don't you stay with Eclipse and keep him calm," Clint said. "I'll find some wood for a ramp."

"I will," Ben promised.

He climbed up onto the back of the buckboard while Clint went inside the barn. Before long, he had dragged out what used to be the side of a stall. They were able to lay that at the edge of the buckboard, and then anchor it on the ground with some heavy sandbags.

"All right," Clint said to Ben, "let's see if we can get the big boy up."

As it turned out, Eclipse was anxious to get to his feet, and he walked right down the makeshift ramp to the ground.

"That's great, fella," Clint said. "Now let's get you into the barn."

He led Eclipse, who limped along behind him, with Ben bringing up the rear. Inside they walked him to a stall that was large enough for the horse to lie down.

"Let's get you off your feet now, so you can rest," Clint said.

Clint and the Salish got Eclipse down; the horse seemed to take a huge sigh of relief. Zelda came walking in, carrying a basin of water, and some bandages.

"I'm going to re-bandage his wounds," she said. "I put a pot of coffee on in the house for you. When I come back in, I'll cook."

"We'll be waiting for you," Clint said.

He and Ben walked to the house, where Clint poured two cups of coffee from the pot on the stove.

"You saw them?" Ben asked.

"The men riding along with us? Yes."

"They were white men."

"I know," Clint said, "and I think I know who they were."

"Who?"

"A man named Wheeler and his two sons," Clint said. "I met them when they came here to try and buy Zelda's place."

"But, this does not look like the kind of place someone would want to buy."

"I know, it's fallen on hard times," Clint said, "but nevertheless, this Wheeler wants to buy it. And he might be trying to scare Zelda into selling."

"She does not wish to sell?" Ben asked.

"She doesn't."

"Then we will help her keep it?"

"I will," Clint said. "She helped me when I needed it. Whether or not you want to get involved is up to you."

"I would like to stay with your horse until he is well again," Ben said. "That means I will stay and help."

"Good," Clint said, "we'll have to tell Zelda about the men, and then we'll have to set watches in case they want to try something at night."

"If you will give me a rifle, I will stand watch all night," Ben said. "I am an old man, and I do not sleep very well. The spirits from the happy hunting ground come to me in my dreams. I would rather stay awake."

"We'll see about that," Clint said. "If you start staying up for hours on end, you might end up falling into a dreamless sleep."

"That would be good," Ben admitted.

Zelda came in.

"He's bedded down," she said. "I cleaned both wounds, and his fever is almost broken. I also fed him and he ate well. Now I'll cook for the three of us."

"I think Ben and I will go out and have a look," Clint said.

"I think one of you should go out," she agreed, "but one of you should stay behind and tell me what's going on."

Clint looked at the Salish, and then handed him his rifle.

Chapter Eleven

Clint remained seated at the table with another cup of coffee while Ben went outside, and Zelda stayed at the stove. He had a headache, and his bones seemed to be aching from his fall. With Eclipse safe in the barn, and on the mend, Clint was able to give in to his own pain for the moment.

"Look at me," Zelda said.

He realized she was standing next to him and he hadn't noticed she had left the stove.

"What?"

"I wanna see your eyes."

He looked up at her and she examined him closely.

"Your eyes ain't right," she said. "I think you need some more time in bed."

He studied her in return, trying to see if she meant bed for sex or sleep. She was serious, talking about sleep.

"Let's wait until Ben comes back in and we eat," he said, "and then maybe I'll go ahead. You got any objection to Ben sleeping inside?"

"Why would I?"

"Well, he's an Indian," Clint said. "Some folks don't like Indians sleeping in their homes."

"I don't mind," she said, "but I was thinkin' somebody should spend the night in the barn with your horse, just in case."

"That sounds like a good idea," Clint said. "Maybe Ben and I can take turns. Then he could come in here and sleep in the corner, over there."

"Just as long as he's in the corner," she said, "and you're in my bed."

"No argument from me."

"For now," she said, "you just sit there and wait for your supper."

"Yes, Ma'am."

***

By the time Ben came back inside, the interior of the house was filled with heady aromas from Zelda's stove.

"Ben," Clint said, "come, sit. The food's almost ready."

"First," Zelda said, "wash your hands in my sink."

Ben went to the sink, primed the pump and then washed his hands.

"Did you see anything out there?" Clint asked, when the Salish sat across from him.

"Yes," Ben said, "three men, like before."

"What three men?" Zelda asked. "Like when?"

"Wheeler and his sons," Clint said. "They paced us all the way home."

"They did?" she asked. "Why didn't you tell me?"

"I didn't want you to worry," Clint said.

"I ain't worried about nobody named Wheeler," she said. "I can handle him."

"Good," Clint said.

She came to the table and gave them both a plate filled with venison and vegetables.

"Thank you," Clint said.

Ben just started eating.

She went back to the stove, then returned to the table with a plate for herself. Clint looked over at the stove. Apparently, everything had been prepared in one pot.

"This is great," he told her.

"Thank you," she said, looking across the table at Ben. "He seems to like it."

Ben realized she was talking about him, so he said, "It is good."

"Thank you," she said. "Now, would you like to tell me what those Wheelers were doin' when you saw them?"

"Watching," Ben said. "Just watching."

She looked at Clint.

"On our way back they were riding with us," Clint said. "Like Ben said, just watching."

"What are they watchin' for?" she asked.

"I also asked why they're watching, at all," Clint said. "They could've burned this place down while we were gone."

"They don't wanna burn it," she said, "they wanna buy it."

"Has anyone else asked you to sell?" he asked.

"Not lately," she said.

"When?"

She thought a moment.

"A coupla months ago, maybe," she said. "Two men came to the door and offered me a lot of money."

"Why didn't you take it?" he asked. "Wasn't it enough?"

"To sell my home?" she asked. "Nobody can offer me enough money to do that."

"Okay, well, Wheeler knows something," he said. "Maybe the same men who offered to buy your property also offered to buy his. And then you refused, so he tried to buy your property to sell it to them."

"But . . . why?" she asked.

"Because they know something we don't," Clint said.

"So, how do we find out what that is?" she asked.

"Simple," he said. "We ask them."

Chapter Twelve

When they finished eating they made their watch and sleeping arrangements. Ben agreed to sleep outside with Eclipse. In fact, he preferred that.

"Well," Clint said, "I'll take the last watch, and sit out on the porch with my rifle."

"What are we watchin' for?" Zelda asked.

"Anything out of the ordinary," Clint said.

"That would mean seein' anythin' but dust," she pointed out.

He smiled.

"Even more dust than usual would mean something," he said.

"All right," she said. "Before Ben beds down I'm gonna go out and check on Eclipse. I also need to bed down my mare."

"I help," Ben said.

"Yeah, you will," Zelda said to him, then turned to Clint. "You get yerself into bed. You need some rest."

"Yes, Ma'am."

***

Zelda and Ben went out to the barn. It was already dark, but Ben kept his eyes alert for any movement. He was carrying Clint's rifle.

"Can you see in the dark?" she asked.

"Yes," he said, simply.

"Can all Indians see in the dark?"

"No."

"How come you can?"

"I am a medicine man."

Zelda had a feeling she wasn't going to get any more of an answer than that.

They entered the barn and went to Eclipse's stall. The horse was lying down, breathing evenly, his eyes open. He recognized them, and remained relaxed.

"Atta boy," Zelda said, crouching down next to him. She stroked his neck, both to keep him calm and to feel how hot he was.

"His fever is still down," she said.

"That is good." He was standing by the door, still looking out into the darkness.

"You think they're comin' at night?" she asked.

"I do not know these men," Ben said. "They could come at any time."

"I doubt it," she said. "I know men like the Wheelers. They're gonna wanna know who Clint is first, before they make a move."

"Then they could move against one of us," Ben said, "and ask us."

"That's not a comforting thought," she said, standing up. "I've checked his bandages. He's fine. I'm gonna bed down my mare, now."

Ben nodded.

As she worked, she said, "Maybe you shouldn't sleep out here all alone, if they're gonna come for one of us."

"I will be fine," he said. "They will not be able to sneak up on me."

"How do you know that?" she asked.

"Simple," he said. "They are white men."

"You don't have a high opinion of white men?"

"Only a few," the Salish said.

"Like Clint?"

"Yes."

She finished up with her mare.

"And you?" he asked.

"What about me?"

"You trust him."

"Clint?" She shrugged. "I suppose so. If he was gonna do anythin' untrustworthy to me, he woulda by now."

"And Indians?"

"Well," she said, "I gotta admit I ain't had too many good experiences with Indians."

"The Salish?"

"No experiences with your people," she said. "But I wouldn't judge you by who your people are. I'd judge you by who you are."

"You are a wise woman," he commented.

"And how do you feel about white women?"

He shrugged.

"They are women."

This would have been harsh, she thought, but he hadn't said them that way.

"I'm goin' inside," she said.

"I will stay."

"Do you need anything?" she asked. "More coffee, a blanket?"

He looked over at the lamp she had lit when they first entered.

"I have enough," he said.

He was wearing only a loin cloth, since he had used his own shirt at some point for a bandage.

"There are some blankets back there," she said, "if it gets cold."

He nodded.

"And there'll be coffee on the stove if you wanna come in and get it."

He nodded, again.

"I will watch you walk back until you are inside," he told her.

"Thanks," she said, "I'll take some comfort from that."

He nodded, didn't seem concerned with whether or not she was serious.

Actually, she didn't really know, herself.

Chapter Thirteen

When Zelda got naked and crawled into bed with Clint, he was almost asleep.

"Sorry," she said, snuggling up against him. "We can just go to sleep."

"Okay," he said, putting his arms around her.

"But we'll have to make up for it in the mornin'," she added.

He didn't bother reminding her that he was getting up early to take the last watch. His head was pounding and his limbs were aching.

"Okay," was all he said, again.

She was asleep before he was . . .

***

Four hours later he was able to slip from her grasp, get out of bed, dress and go into the kitchen without waking her. There was an almost full pot of coffee on the stove. He filled two mugs and carried them out to the barn.

As he walked inside Ben suddenly appeared.

"I heard you when you left the house," the Salish said, "but I wanted to make sure."

"No harm there," Clint said, handing the man a mug of coffee.

Ben accepted it with a nod of thanks.

"See or hear anything?" Clint asked.

"No," Ben said, "no one has come near tonight."

"I don't know what the Wheelers are waiting for," Clint said.

"The lady said they are waiting to see who you are," Ben explained.

"When they came to the door, I didn't introduce myself. Maybe I should've . . ."

"I will see you in the morning," Ben said, and left the barn.

Zelda's comment showed what a smart woman she was. It also showed Clint that he still was not thinking clearly. If not for the Wheelers hanging around he could get more sleep, which would probably clear his head.

Usually when he was on watch he had Eclipse to back him, but one look at the Darley Arabian showed that he was fast asleep.

At least one of them was on his way to a fast recovery.

***

Before Clint could make his way back to the house as the sun came up, Zelda appeared with a fresh cup of coffee.

"Thanks," he said, accepting it gratefully.

"Bacon-and-eggs in a few minutes," she said. "Biscuits and spuds with it."

"Sounds great," he said. "Is Ben up?"

"Awake and sittin' on the porch with your rifle."

"That's good to know," Clint said. "He's a good man."

"How long have you known him?" she asked.

"He just came along after Eclipse and I had our fall," Clint explained. "Offered to help."

"That does sound like a good man," she said.

"I think he was more concerned about Eclipse than he was about me," Clint said, "but that's okay."

"Well, he patched you both up," she said. "That makes him okay in my book. Come on inside in about ten minutes and we can eat."

"I'll be there."

As she left, Clint walked over to Eclipse's stall, which was the biggest one in the barn, with a swinging door on it. As he got to the door and looked over it, he saw that the Darley had made his way to his feet.

"Well," Clint said, "you must be feeling better."

The inured front leg was straight, and the horse's weight was on it.

"You're looking good, big boy," Clint said. "We'll be back on the trail in no time."

The big Darley just stared at him.

"I'm going in the house for breakfast," Clint said. "See you later."

***

As Clint headed for the house, the Wheelers were having breakfast in their own house, served by Hattie Wheeler, Kent's wife and mother to the boys.

"When are we gonna do somethin', Pa?" Dave, the oldest, asked.

"As soon as we know who we're dealin' with," Wheeler said. "If Zelda brought in a gunfighter—"

"Oh, hell, you think she'd do that? Hattie asked, interrupting her man. "She's more likely to pick up a rifle and fill you full of holes herself."

"You ain't gonna let 'er do that, are ya, Pa?" Leonard asked.

"Of course not!"

"Then what do we do?" Dave asked.

"You shut up," their mother said, "and eat!"

"We could—" Kent started, but he was cut off by his loving wife.

"All of ya!"

Chapter Fourteen

Clint had a few pieces of bacon, leaving most of it for Zelda and Ben. On the other hand, Zelda had one or two, leaving the rest for the Salish. There were plenty of biscuits to fill them up.

"What are you gonna do today?" Zelda asked.

"You and Ben are going to stay here and keep an eye on Eclipse—and each other."

"And what are you gonna do?" Zelda repeated.

"I'm going to introduce myself to the Wheelers," he said.

"How will you get there?" Ben asked.

"I'll saddle Zelda's mare, if she'll let me."

"Of course," Zelda said, "but don't push her too hard."

"Only as far as the Wheeler's live," he promised, "if you'll direct me."

"I can do that."

They finished breakfast, and then Ben went out to the barn to check on Eclipse, and saddle the mare.

Zelda told Clint how to get to the Wheeler ranch.

"Don't stick to the road," she said. "If you ride the way I tell you, you can shorten the journey by an hour—

but it'll still take two on my mare. If you wait, don't you think they'll come here again?"

"Probably," Clint said, "but I'll throw them off balance by going there."

"And what if, while you go there, they come here?" she asked.

"If they're watching," Clint said, "I think they'll follow me."

"And once they realize where you're going? Won't they stop you?"

"They might," he said. "And that would shorten my ride, wouldn't it? On the other hand, Ben didn't see any sign of them during the night, and I didn't see them this morning. I might be able to get to the ranch while they're still home. How ever it goes, I'll find them or they'll find me."

"Are you countin' on them knowin' who you are?"

"Do you know who I am?"

"Well, sure I do," she said. "You told me your name, and I recognized it."

"Then so will they."

She sighed.

"I hope you know what you're doin'," she said. "You're not fully recovered yet. I wouldn't want you to get hurt again tryin' to help me."

"Hey, I didn't like Wheeler and his sons when they were here," he said. "I think it's time for me to tell them that."

"Just come back in one piece," she said. "That's all I ask."

"I'm going to do my best."

***

After breakfast at the Wheeler ranch Hattie pulled her husband aside.

"You ain't goin' to Zelda's place today."

"We got to," he said. "We got to show her she can't get away with hirin' help against us."

"You and your boys got chores to do around here," she said. "You wanna go over there and fight some man you don't even know, do it after that."

"All right, woman!" he snapped. "The chores will get done."

She softened.

"Kent, if we're gonna sell this place it's gotta look like it's worth somethin'," she said.

"And that's why we gotta buy Zelda's ranch," he told her. "To fix it up, too."

"Why don't you just go there and fix it up for her, like a good neighbor?" she asked.

"I ain't tryin' to be a good neighbor," he said. "I'm tryin' to make money!"

"Well then, get out there and make this place look like it's worth somethin'."

***

Clint walked to the barn, where Ben had Zelda's mare saddled and ready to go.

"Do you want me to come with you?" the Salish asked.

"No," Clint said. "I want you to stay here and look out for Eclipse—and Zelda."

Clint mounted the mare.

"Do you want your rifle?" Ben asked, holding it out.

"No," Clint said, "hold onto it."

Clint rode the mare outside, with Ben walking alongside them.

"If those men come here," Ben said.

"The Wheelers?"

"Yes," Ben said. "Do you want me to kill them?"

Clint looked at the old Salish, and had no doubt that he would have done just that—or die trying.

"No," Clint said, "don't kill them. Just keep them from hurting Zelda—or my horse."

Chapter Fifteen

The mare was solid, and a good buckboard horse, but she clearly wasn't comfortable with a saddle on her back. But after half an hour, Clint had managed to find a comfortable gait and let her go at her own pace which, luckily, was more than a walk.

He didn't see anyone near Zelda's ranch, and as he left her property, nobody made a move to intercept him. So he was fairly sure the Wheelers would be home when he got there.

As he came within sight of a house, he knew from Zelda's description that it was the Wheeler place. The house was similar to Zelda's, except that it had been kept up. The same was true for the corral and barn. He decided to play it straight, and rode right up to the house. Before he could even dismount, a woman came out of the house and pointed a rifle at him.

She was a handsome, middle-aged woman with long black hair streaked with grey. She was wearing a blue homemade dress made of some thin cotton. The rifle in her hands was a Winchester, and it didn't tremble once.

"Who are ya and whataya want?"

"My name's Clint Adams," he said, "and I want to talk."

The woman smiled and became pretty.

"Yer the Gunsmith."

"That's right."

"Guess I can put this down," she said, lowering the rifle. "You can probably draw and kill me before I could pull the trigger."

"I'd prefer not to do that."

"You the feller chased my boys away from Zelda's place?" she asked.

"I wasn't aware I chased them."

"Guess I oughtta be glad you didn't kill them, neither," she commented.

"I don't want to do that," he told her.

"Ya wanna come in fer a cup of coffee?" she asked.

"Now that I can do," he said, looking around before dismounting.

"Don't worry," she said. "My boys are out with my husband doin' chores. Ain't gonna be back for hours." She grinned. "We got us all the time in the world to get acquainted."

He followed her into the house.

***

Later, while she was on her knees under the table, sucking his cock, he remembered what she said about having time to "get acquainted." He didn't think this was what she meant.

But there they were, he with his pants down around his ankles, and her with his hard cock in her mouth—and her "boys" not due back for hours . . .

***

"Black and strong, right?" she'd asked as they entered the house.

"How did you know?"

"You're that kind of man," she said.

He looked around. Most of the furniture looked handmade. The kitchen table and chairs were very sturdy.

"Your husband do all this work on the furniture?" he asked.

"Oh no," she said, with her back to him. "That's me." Then she turned her head to look at him. "Have a seat."

She brought the coffee to the table, set it down in front of him. She had left her rifle by the stove.

"You know," he said, as she sat across from him, "if you hadn't told me you were their mother, I would've thought you were Dave and Leonard's older sister."

"Ah, you're a flatterer."

"Not at all," he said. "You don't look old enough to be the mother of two grown boys."

She sipped her coffee, then dried her lips with her fingers and said, "For that I should give you a suck."

"What?"

"Before I got married, I was a whore," she said. "And a damned good one."

"Mrs. Wheeler—"

"My name's Hattie."

"Hattie—"

"Would you like a suck?"

"I—what?"

"I mean, do you like it when a woman sucks your tallywacker?"

"Well, yeah, but—"

That was when she slid under the table.

"Hattie—"

"Just sit still," she said. "Here, put your gun on the table. I know you'll want to keep it close."

With his gun on the table and his pants around his ankles, she went on to prove just how good a whore she had been. She sucked him, wetly, until he was nice and hard, then both sucked and pumped him with one hand until he shot a load into her mouth, which she swallowed with no trouble.

"There, see?"

Suddenly, she was back in the chair across from him, drying her lips with her fingers, as she had done when she sipped her coffee. Both the sip and suck were all the same to her, apparently.

He pulled his trousers back up and strapped his gun back on.

"You didn't fight me on that," she said. "Why not?"

"It might have upset the table," he said, "and spilled the coffee."

"You didn't want to insult me," she said. "You want me to keep talkin' to you."

"That's right."

She touched her lips again.

"You tasted really good."

"Thank you."

She pushed her coffee cup away. Apparently, the suck had tasted better than the sip.

"Would you like to see me naked?" she asked.

"Would you like me to see you naked?"

"Very much."

"Are you trying to keep me busy until your husband and sons can get here?"

"No," she said, "my husband is terrible in bed. He fucks me, then rolls over and goes to sleep. It occurs to me you're not like that."

"I'm not."

"Well then . . ."

She stood up and shrugged off her dress. For a woman who was middle-aged and had given birth to children, she had a fine body. Slender, with high, peach-sized breasts that should have been sagging at her age, but weren't. A trim waist that should have been carrying some extra meat, but wasn't. Her belly was a little soft, and showed the stretch marks of child birth, but otherwise was smooth. Her hips were wide and, as she turned, he saw butt cheeks that were smooth and only slightly sagged. All-in-all his cock was standing again, even though she had just sucked him dry.

"So," he said, "the bedroom?"

"Oh no," she said, "not in the bed where I sleep with my husband. Right here." She knocked on the table. "I'll move the cups."

"What if your husband—" he said, as she took the cups away and came back.

"I'm gonna lie on this table so that I can see out the window," she said. "Don't worry, if they come back, I'll see 'em."

With that she hopped up on the table, laid back and spread her legs, showing him the heavy pubic patch between her thighs.

"Come on," she said, "you can't fuck me while you're dressed."

He stripped down, hung his gun belt on the back of his chair, and then moved it so he could stand in front of her. This was the last thing he had expected when he left Zelda's, but he found himself very much looking forward to driving himself into her.

When he did it, it was with no resistance, since she was already soaking wet. She gasped as he pierced her to the hilt, then he took hold of her knees and started pumping in and out of her. The sturdy table beneath them took all their weight with no trouble. For a moment he found himself wondering if she had done this before—with a neighbor. A hand? A drummer? —but then he got involved in what he was doing and stopped thinking.

He leaned over so he could take her breasts into his mouth, found them amazingly firm. He wondered what she had done all these years to keep them that way.

"Oh yeah," she said, "that's it, that's what I want, come on, harder . . . faster . . ." It became more difficult for her to speak as he did give it to her harder and faster and her breathing became labored.

The table continued to bear their weight, but started to move across the floor as he fucked her. He felt his own explosion starting to build in his legs, when suddenly she went rigid, and then began to thrash about beneath him. First her eyes went wide with shock, surprise or both, and then she closed them tight, just as her vagina seemed to do the same on his cock. It suddenly felt like her insides were milking him, and he let go, exploding inside her and continuing to ejaculate as the feeling went from pleasure to pain and back again . . .

***

"No sign of them," she said, dressing in front of the window as she stared out. Then she turned to face him, with her dress buttoned up. "I don't know what you really came here to do, Adams, but I'm just as hell glad you came."

Strapping his gun back on he said, "I'm glad you approve, Hattie . . . and just call me Clint."

"Well," she said, "if you don't mind, I'll call you Adams when my husband and sons get back. No need for them to know we got . . . friendly."

"I understand."

"More coffee?" she asked.

"If you think we'll be able to sit at that table and just drink it," he said.

She smiled.

"Don't you worry," she said. "You done satisfied me for a long time. Now I'll be able to put up with my husband's ruttin' and snortin' and sleepin' for a few years more."

"Happy to be of service."

"Service?" she asked, placing two cups of coffee down on the table. "I ain't reacted like that during' sex in a long time."

"You mean . . . that used to happen when you were . . ."

"Whorin'? Once in a while there'd be a man who fit me just right, and yeah, it would happen . . . but I don't remember them feelin's goin' through me for that long."

"I'm glad I could bring back some good memories for you," he said.

"You didn't just bring 'em back, Mister," she said, "you gave me some new ones. Uh-oh."

"What?"

She got up and walked to the stove, picked up her rifle and pointed it at him.

"Here they come," she said. "If ya don't mind, I want them to think I held this on you the whole time."

He looked out the window, saw three riders coming, then looked back at Hattie, who now seemed like a completely different woman from the one who had just been naked on the table.

Chapter Sixteen

They remained that way until the three men dismounted, and two of them came through the door.

"Just unsaddle 'em, Leonard, and stop complainin'," the father was saying as they entered.

"He's the youngest," Dave said, "he's gotta do more—"

"Shut up, damn—"

They both stopped talking when they saw Clint sitting at the table. Clint noticed they weren't armed, which was good. But Hattie was still holding the rifle on him.

"What's he doin' here?" Wheeler demanded of his wife.

"Said he come to see you," Hattie said. "I thought I'd hold 'im here for you."

"You got a name, friend?" Kent Wheeler asked.

"Clint Adams."

Wheeler let that sink in, then looked at his wife and waved a hand.

"Put that rifle up, mother," he said. "This feller could draw and kill you before you even pulled the trigger. This here's the Gunsmith."

"Well," Hattie said, lowering her rifle, "whataya know?"

Clint thought the Hattie Wheeler he knew was somebody he'd never call "mother."

"What did she give you? Coffee? Dave, get the squeezin's."

Dave went across the kitchen and picked up a jug, brought it back. Kent Wheeler sat down across from Clint, uncorked the jug and chugged some.

"This is real good moonshine," he said, pushing the jug over to Clint.

Clint picked it up, tipped it and drank. It burned its way down his throat and spread out through his body. He shoved the jug back at Wheeler.

"Now, suppose you tell me why Zelda went out and got herself a gunfighter?"

"I'm not a gunfighter," Clint said.

"Ain't that your reputation?"

"I have reputations for all kinds of different things," Clint said. "But gunfighter usually means gun for sale, and I don't sell mine."

"Then whataya doin' here, Mr. Gunsmith?"

He explained about falling, the walk, and waking up in Zelda's house.

"She was nice enough to take me in and patch me up," Clint said.

"So you're not workin' for her?"

"No."

"Then why are ya here?" Wheeler asked. "Ya wanna work for me?"

"No, I don't."

"Then I'll ask ya again, why are ya here?"

"I just came to introduce myself," Clint said. "After all, we didn't really get properly introduced at Zelda's house."

At that point the door opened and Leonard came walking in, not looking happy.

"There I did it—" he started, then saw Clint. "What's he doin' here?"

"Relax," Kent Wheeler said to his son. "Mr. Adams came to introduce himself."

"Adams?"

"Clint Adams," Dave said. "The Gunsmith."

Leonard's eyes got big. "Really?"

"So how long will you be stickin' around" Wheeler asked.

Clint stood up, at that point and faced the three Wheeler men. Hattie remained standing by her stove, having leaned the rifle against it.

"I'll be here until you forget about trying to buy Zelda's ranch."

"And why would I do that?" Wheeler asked, standing. His sons moved to either side of him.

"Because she doesn't want to sell," Clint said.

"Maybe she doesn't know she wants to sell," Wheeler offered.

"And you're going to make her realize it?"

"I just have to make the right offer," Wheeler said.

"Why don't you tell me why you want to buy her place?" Clint asked.

"I'm lookin' ta make my empire bigger," Kent said, and the boys chuckled.

"Why?"

Kent looked over at Hattie, who stared back at him with no expression.

"I got a wife who wants me to better myself."

Clint looked at Hattie, who rolled her eyes.

"So you're going to keep making offers?"

"Better and better ones, until she says yes."

"And you weren't planning to try and scare her when I saw you at the house?"

"Why would I try to scare a woman?" Kent asked.

His boys chuckled again but he silenced them with a look.

"I can tell you," Clint said, "she's not going to sell. Not without a real good reason."

"And what would you do if she said yes?"

"If she says yes," Clint replied, "I'll be on my way as soon as my horse is able. But until then, I'm going to be around."

From behind her three men Hattie smiled and blew Clint a kiss.

He backed his way to the door, and left.

***

"How long was he here?" Wheeler demanded of his wife.

"About ten minutes before you got here," she said. "Should I have shot him?"

Wheeler grinned nastily.

"You never woulda got a shot off, woman," he said. "Now fix some food for me and my boys!"

"My pleasure," she said, but she didn't mean cooking for them. She meant how her legs still felt weak from the fucking Clint Adams had given her on the table the Wheeler men were now sitting at.

Chapter Seventeen

Clint didn't push the mare on the way back to Zelda's. After all, there was no hurry. He passed a water hole on the way, where he let the mare drink to her heart's content while he removed his shirt and tried to wash the smell of Hattie Wheeler off of him. It was his experience that a woman could always smell another woman on a man.

When he was done, he mounted the mare again and continued on to Zelda's. Having not pushed the mare, by the time he arrived he had been gone over six hours. It was quiet when he rode up to the barn, dismounted and entered. Suddenly he found a rifle barrel poking out at him from his right.

"It's me," he said.

"I see," Ben said, lowering the rifle. "I just wanted to make sure."

"Everything okay here?" Clint asked.

"Eclipse is fine."

"And Zelda?"

"She is inside." Ben shrugged. "I think she is all right."

"And you?" Clint asked. "Are you okay?"

"Yes. How did your meeting with the Wheelers go?" Ben asked.

"Come inside," Clint said, "I'll tell you and Zelda at the same time. But first, let's get this mare unsaddled."

***

When they walked in, Zelda was sitting at the kitchen table. She looked up and smiled.

"You're back," she said.

"I am."

"Coffee?"

"Sure."

She got up and went to the stove. As she came back with the cups she said, "I see you're not dead. Is anybody else?"

"No," Clint said.

"Was Wheeler there?"

"They were all there," Clint said. "Kent, Dave, Leonard and . . . Hattie."

"Hattie's not a bad girl," Zelda said. "But her men folk? They're animals. And her boys are stupid."

"I noticed that."

She had put three cups of coffee on the table. Ben walked over and silently sat, so that they were now all seated. But Clint sat so he could look out the windows.

"So what did you find out?" she asked.

He took his eyes from the window and looked at her.

"Kent Wheeler is going to keep offering to buy this place until you agree."

"Really?" she asked. "Where is he gonna get that much money?"

"I don't know."

"Did he say why he wants to buy it?"

"He wants to expand his empire, because he has a wife who wants him to better himself."

"Crap."

"That's what I thought."

"What did you tell him?"

"That I'd be around until he either stopped bothering you, or until you decided to sell."

"Good," she said. "That means you're gonna be around here for a long time." She looked at the Salish. "What about you, Ben? You wanna stay around here?"

"I will stay to help," he said.

"That's good, too," she said.

"And while we're here," Clint said, "we might as well do some work."

"What did you have in mind?" she asked.

"General repairs," he said. "The other corral, the barn, the house."

"That'll work," she said.

"But we'll need to take your buckboard to the nearest town for supplies."

"I think," she said, "if you look behind the barn, you'll find what you need."

"You have the supplies for repairs?" he asked.

She nodded.

"I just never seem to get around to it."

Chapter Eighteen

Clint and Ben walked around behind the barn, saw stacks of building materials covered by tarpaulins.

"She wasn't kidding," Clint said, looking under the tarps. "There's plenty of wood here for repairs on the barn, and posts for fencing and the corral."

"I do not know how to do those things," Ben said.

"That's okay," Clint said. "While I do the repairs, you're going to be on watch. And you'll also be checking on Eclipse."

The Indian nodded.

"I can do those things."

"Good." Clint tossed the tarp completely off the first stack of wood. "I'll need to find Zelda's tools."

"Tools?"

"Hammers, nails, shovel . . ."

"I saw those things in the barn," Ben told him.

"Then let's go and get them."

Clint followed Ben into the barn, and to the back where there were some shelves.

"Is that what you want?" Ben asked, pointing.

Clint saw the hammer, nails, shovels, and other tools that would be necessary for all the repairs.

"That's them."

It was getting too dark to start any work, so they went back into the house, which was filled with the aromas from Zelda's cooking.

The meal this time was chicken and potatoes. This was the first time Clint noticed that she had a chicken coop out back. He hoped, after another night's sleep, that all his mental powers would be back. For a man like him, with a reputation that drew an invisible target on his back, not being alert could be the death of him.

Ben wolfed down his food without comment, but that was enough of a compliment for Zelda.

After they finished eating, Ben stood up and said, "I will go and stay with the horse."

"I'll be there later," Clint said.

Ben went out the door, leaving Zelda and Clint alone.

"How did you like the food?"

"It was great, as always."

"So do you want to thank me?" she asked, with a twinkle in her eyes.

"I do," he said, but since he wasn't sure he was completely recovered from being with Hattie that afternoon, he said, "But let's save that for bed tonight."

"With Ben in the other room?"

He grinned at her.

"Let's see how quiet you can be."

"You're a mean man," she said. "Tell me, did Hattie try to show you her whoring skills?"

"Whoring?" he asked.

"She was a whore before Wheeler brought her back here and married her."

"We didn't get that far," he said. "I was there ten minutes before Wheeler and his boys walked in."

"Good thing," she said. "They might've walked in on somethin'."

"Well," he said, "I'm going to have to be careful if I see her again."

"Yeah," she said, "try not to be alone with her for too long."

"I'll keep that in mind," he said. "But right now I'm going out to check on Eclipse."

"That animal means a lot to you, doesn't he?"

"He does," Clint said, "and I hope I mean a lot to him. "We're partners."

"Well," she said, "go and see to your partner."

He could tell by the way she was looking at him that she didn't know whether to believe him or not about Hattie Wheeler.

***

When Ben left the house, he walked slowly to the barn, keeping his eyes and ears open. He didn't see anything, but he thought he heard movement. He stopped just outside the barn, stood still and listened.

Someone was out in the darkness moving around, and it wasn't white men.

***

Clint left the house and started for the barn. Halfway there he paused, then continued on more slowly. When he entered the barn, Ben looked at him with serious eyes.

"Who's out there?" Clint asked.

"Not white men."

"What tribes are in the area?" Clint asked.

"Could be Crow, could be Cheyenne."

"Not your people?"

"No."

"What are they going to want?" Clint asked.

"Could be just to trade," Ben said, "could be your horse."

"Well, I'll trade with them," Clint said, "but they're not getting Eclipse."

"And the woman?"

Clint didn't hesitate.

"They're not getting her, either."

Chapter Nineteen

"Will you tell Zelda?" Ben asked.

"I haven't decided," Clint said. "I don't want to worry her."

"She has lived here a long time," Ben said. "She might know more about them than you do."

"That's a good point," Clint said. "I guess I better go tell her and see what she has to say."

"I will stay around here, tonight," Ben said.

"I'll let you know what she says," Clint assured him.

Clint stopped at Eclipse's stall first, saw the horse standing there, seemingly putting all his weight on the injured leg.

"How you doing, big fella?" Clint asked.

The Darley nodded his head up and down, as if telling Clint he was fine. Then he pawed the ground with the hoof of his injured leg, as if asking when they were going to get out and run?

"Pretty soon," he assured Eclipse, patting him on the neck.

He left the barn after that and headed back to the house.

"Why do you have that look on your face?" Zelda asked, as he entered.

"Let's sit at the table."

"What's wrong? Is your horse all right?"

"He's fine."

"Is Ben okay?"

"Ben's fine," Clint said. "Just sit. I want to talk to you."

She sat across from him.

"First, Ben's going to stay out in the barn with Eclipse tonight."

"Ah," she said, "that's good news. I won't have to keep quiet."

"Don't forget he's got great hearing," Clint said. "In fact, that's the other thing."

"What?"

"There's somebody out in the dark," Clint said, "and Ben says it's not white men."

"More Indians?"

"He says Crow or Cheyenne," Clint said. "You've lived here a long time. Have you ever traded with them?"

"We traded with some Cree while my husband was alive," she said. "and I might have given some meat to a few Cheyenne over the years."

"They never threatened you?"

"No," she said. "What do you think they're after?"

"It could be Eclipse," Clint said.

"I can believe that," she commented. "I've never seen another horse like him."

"Well," Clint said, "Ben will be out there all night and if he hears anything, he'll fire a shot."

"Maybe they'll show themselves in the mornin'," she said, "and we can find out what they want."

"That would be the way I'd like it to go," Clint admitted. He didn't tell her about the question Ben had asked him concerning who he would give up, her or Eclipse. Since he had no intention of giving either up, there was no point in discussing it.

Hopefully.

"It's early," she said, "but you could start thankin' me now."

She stood up and started to unbutton her dress. Before she took it off, however, she walked to the bedroom door. There she dropped the dress to the floor just before she darted into the room.

"I'm waitin'!" she called out.

He sighed, stood and headed for the bedroom door, hoping his performance would not be hindered by his energetic afternoon.

***

"I thought we were goin' over to Zelda's ranch today," Leonard complained.

"We had work to do on our own place," Kent Wheeler told him. "We'll take a ride over there tomorrow."

"Are you afraid of the Gunsmith, Pa?" Dave asked.

"No, I ain't afraid of him!"

They were outside on the porch, drinking whiskey after supper.

"Are you afraid of Ma?" Dave asked, smiling.

"Of course I am!" Wheeler said. "Every man needs to be afraid of his woman. You boys would do well to keep that in mind for the future."

"My woman's gonna keep her mouth shut and her legs open," Leonard said.

"You got a lot to learn boy!" Wheeler said. "You better keep your mouth shut and learn it!"

"Yes, Pa."

"You got anythin' else to say?" Wheeler demanded of his oldest, Dave.

"No, Pa."

"That's good," Wheeler said. "Make sure the stock's all bedded down, both of ya."

"Yes, Pa."

Wheeler went into the house, where his wife was cleaning the kitchen after supper.

"You expect me ta believe you didn't give the Gun-smith a poke while he was here?"

She turned and looked at him, smiling.

"Well, of course I gave him a poke," she said. "But first I sucked him. I was doin' whatever I could to keep him here for you."

Wheeler turned red.

"You shoulda walked in here with a gun and took care of him," she said, putting her hands on her hips. "The three of ya. Now we gotta deal with him to get that place away from Zelda."

"*I* gotta deal with him," Wheeler said. "You're gonna stay away from him from now on!"

"Is that right?"

He unbuckled his trousers and dropped them to his ankles. He wasn't wearing any underwear, and a massive erection was jutting out at her.

"This is the only thing you're gonna suck!" he told her.

She stared down at it, thick and veiny and ugly, not pretty like the Gunsmith's.

"What if the boys come in?"

"They're beddin' down the stock," he told her. "Now get to it, woman. I gotta clean out your mouth from what you did today with Adams."

She sighed, left her dress on just in case the boys did come in, and got down on her knees in front of her husband.

Chapter Twenty

Clint pressed his face to Zelda's pubic patch and worked on her with his tongue until she was soaking the bottom half of his face with her juices.

"Oh yeah, yeah, yeah," she said, grabbing his head, "right there . . ." She began moving her hips, rubbing herself against his face. Then she started to tremble, almost uncontrollably, but kept rubbing her crotch into his face until the trembling stopped.

"Oooh, God," she said, as he settled onto his back next to her, "it's been years . . ."

"I'm glad to be of help," he said. "I still owe you."

"And I'm gonna keep collectin'," she said, reaching down and grabbing his hard cock.

She slithered down until she was between his thighs, then began to lick the length of his erection. When she had it good and wet, she took it into her mouth and began to suck.

He held her head the way she had held his, and moved his hips in rhythm with her sucking action. She used her hands as well as her mouth, and before long he was grunting as he tried to keep from yelling. He didn't want Ben to come running in . . .

***

"We did good," she said later, lying with her head on his shoulder—the left shoulder. "Ben didn't hear a sound."

"Hopefully," he said, "nobody did."

"You still think there are Indians out there in the dark?" she asked.

"There's a strong possibility," he said. "I sensed somebody, but Ben heard them. I trust his hearing."

"Do you trust him to stand by your side if they come in?" she asked.

"Do you think he would join them?"

"I don't know," she said. "What if they're Salish."

"He claims they won't be his people."

"But what if they are?" she questioned.

"I guess we'll have to wait and see what happens then," he answered.

"I'm tired," she said. "Can we go to sleep?"

"We can," he said.

But as she drifted off quickly, he did so slowly, thinking about the questions she had asked. What if the Indians came in the morning, and they were Salish?

What would Ben do?

***

Ben stood at the barn door with Clint's rifle in his hand, listening intently. He could hear the wind, and the dirt that the wind was moving. He also heard the sounds men make when they're trying to keep quiet. He could pick up footfalls on the sand, even if they were being made by bare feet. And, of course, the sound of their ponies.

They were out there.

He had told Clint that they wouldn't be his people, Salish, in truth he wasn't sure. But even if they were, they had put him out. If they came with the daylight, he would stand with Clint in defense of the horse, and the woman.

No matter what.

***

Once again Clint was able to slip out of bed without waking Zelda. She was either a very sound sleeper, or the sex put her under. Either way, he was able to don his trousers and walk to the other part of the house.

There was hot coffee on the stove, so he poured himself a cup, then sat at the table so he'd be able to see out the windows—one on either side of the front door.

Chapter Twenty-One

When morning came he crawled back into bed with Zelda, so she wouldn't know he had been in the kitchen most of the night. He had dozed off a few times there, but for the most part had been awake, watching.

Zelda woke and stretched.

"Did you sleep good?" she asked.

"Like death," he said.

"Me, too," she said. "Best sleep I've had in years, thanks to you."

He rolled over and kissed her. She reached for his crotch, but he rolled away.

"No, no," he said, "we've got to be ready for anything, this morning."

"And that means a good breakfast," she said. She leaped out of bed and stretched her taut body. He watched for a moment, then turned and got himself dressed.

As she started breakfast, he left the house and walked to the barn. Ben was standing in the doorway when he got there.

"Been there all night?"

Ben nodded.

"Seen anything?"

"No."

"Heard anything?"

"A lot."

"Like what?" Clint asked.

"Footsteps, from men, horses," Ben said.

"Boots?"

"Bare feet, moccasins."

"So definitely Indians."

"Yes."

Clint looked out over the horizon, saw nothing. He was going to have to depend on Ben's hearing.

"Well," he said, "it's light, now. If they're going to come, it'll be soon."

"Yes," Ben said.

"And if they're Salish?"

Ben looked at him.

"I am with you," he said, "not them."

"Good," Clint said. "We better go back to the house for breakfast."

That brightened Ben's eyes. He was really enjoying Zelda's cooking.

"Yes!" he said.

Clint took a quick look at Eclipse, then both he and Ben headed back to the house, keeping alert. They had no way of knowing whether or not someone was going to send a bullet or an arrow to announce themselves.

Zelda greeted them with coffee, flapjacks and bacon.

As usual Ben sat down and dug in.

Clint and Zelda sat across from each other and while Ben wolfed down his food, Clint told her what the Salish had told him.

"But no sign of them?" she asked.

"Not yet."

"What do we do when they come?" she asked.

"We talk to them."

"I have a rifle—" she started.

"No," Clint said, "no weapon for you. You'll just go out and see if they want to trade. Ben and I will be at the windows with rifles."

"I'm not exactly comfortable with that," she admitted, "but okay. I'll do it your way."

Ben looked at Clint.

"You never answered my question," the Salish said.

"Ben—" Clint said, warningly.

"Will you give them the horse, or her?" he asked, pointing at Zelda.

"What?"

"He thinks they may want my horse, or they may want you."

Ben smiled at Zelda and nodded.

"And what would you do?" she asked.

"I'd give them my horse, of course," he told her.

"You would?"

"Yes," he said, "and then I'd go and get him back."

"I go with you," Ben said.

Zelda looked at him and smiled again.

"This food is good," he said.

"Thank you."

Clint was looking out the window, when he saw them in the distance.

"Okay," he said, "this is it."

"What?"

Ben and Zelda both looked out the window.

"Who is it?" she asked.

Ben stared a few more minutes as they got closer, then said, "Five braves."

"Five?"

"Cheyenne?" Clint asked.

"Crow," Ben answered.

Clint would've preferred Cheyenne. They were generally considered a civilized tribe.

"All right," Clint said, "maybe one of us should go out with Zelda to talk to them."

"No," Zelda said, "let's stick to the original plan. I doubt they'll do anythin' to me right off. They'll talk first."

"Ben?" Clint asked.

"I agree with her."

"All right, then," Clint said. "Go on out, Zelda. But wait until they get closer. No point in letting them know we spotted them early."

"Okay."

She walked to the front door, took a deep breath and stood there, waiting for the word from Clint.

"Ben, get by that window," Clint said, pointing to the one on the right. "Keep that rifle handy, but stay out of sight for now."

Ben nodded and moved.

"Zelda, if it comes to it and you feel threatened, go ahead and tell them there's a rifle in each window, pointed at them. We'll let them see us, then."

"Okay."

Clint moved to the window on the left, kept out of sight while watching the five Crow Indians approach. He didn't see any rifles.

"Okay, Zelda," he said "Go!"

Chapter Twenty-Two

Zelda stepped out of the house, her hands in the pockets of her apron, as the Crow approach.

"Where is your man?" one Crow asked.

"My man is dead," she said. "He died a long time ago."

"You live alone?" he asked. He was sitting dead center, with two Crow on his right, and two on his left.

"Yes."

He studied her.

"You are sturdy woman."

"Thank you."

"You would make good squaw."

"No," she said, "I don't think I would."

He frowned.

"You have two men here with you," he said. "They work for you?"

"They do, yeah."

"Where are they?"

"They're around."

All five Crow glanced around, then looked intently at the house. The center Crow looked at her, again.

"We trade."

"All right. What do you want?"

"We want to trade with your men," the Crow said. "We have good ponies, trade for you."

"Me?"

"I want you for squaw. You are sturdy woman, good worker," he said. "Little Bear want you for squaw."

"Well, Little Bear," she said, "I gotta tell you, that ain't gonna happen. You can trade for anything else. Meat, blankets, tools—"

"Woman," Little Bear said. "I want woman."

"No."

"I trade with men," he said. "Call them."

"They're here," she said. "They're pointing rifles at you from the windows."

The Crow braves all sat up straight. Three got their bows ready, one tightened his grip on his lance. Little Bear just stared.

"There is no need for guns," he said. "We trade."

"Little Bear—" she started, but then the door opened behind her.

***

"They want woman," Ben said, "not horse."

"Maybe they don't know about the horse," Clint said, as the Crow brave conversed with Zelda.

"Maybe don't care," Ben said. "He want squaw. She make good one."

"Yes, she would," Clint said, "but she's not going with him."

Clint moved toward the door.

"Stay at the window, Ben," he instructed. "Don't fire unless I do."

Ben just nodded.

Clint opened the door and stepped out.

***

When Zelda heard the door open behind her she breathed a sigh of relief.

She saw Little Bear look past her at Clint, and his eyes narrowed. Did he recognize Clint? Was the Gunsmith as well known among the Indians, she wondered?

As Clint stepped up right next to her she took great comfort from her arm touching his.

His left one, of course. She already knew that he always had to keep his gun arm free. And then she was thrilled by his first words.

"I am her man!"

Chapter Twenty-Three

"The woman said she had no man!" Little Bear challenged.

"I claim her," Clint said. "From this day forward, she will be my woman."

The Crow brave pounded his chest.

"Little Bear claims her!" he snapped.

"Then let the woman choose her own man," Clint said.

Little bear exchanged glances with his braves, a derisive look on a face that was as chiseled as his chest. He looked as if he had been carved out of stone, and seemed to only be in his twenties. An excellent specimen of manhood that Clint had no desire to go up against, hand-to-hand, but he had the feeling that was what it was coming to.

"A squaw does not claim her own man," he said, as if Clint had said something totally crazy.

"This one does!" Zelda said. She reached a hand out to touch Clint. "And I choose him."

Little Bear pointed his finger at Clint.

"You want her?"

"Yes."

"Then you will fight me for her!"

Clint knew he could draw and fire, killing at least three of the braves, while Ben would probably take care of the other two. But he didn't want to kill 5 men.

Of course, he didn't want one of them to kill him.

"You challenge me?" Clint asked.

"Yes," the man said, "Little Bear challenges you."

"Then I choose the weapons."

"You accept?"

"If I can choose the weapons."

"And if I do not agree to that?" Little Bear asked, with a smile.

"Then I'll kill you and your braves, right now, with my gun," Clint said.

"You think you can kill five of us?" Little Bear asked. "Before we kill you?"

"I know I can."

Clint was holding his rifle in his left hand, and his right was hanging down by his holstered gun.

"You have guns," Little Bear said, spreading his arms. "We do not."

"And that's why I know I can do it."

After a moment's hesitation Little Bear asked, "What weapons do you choose?"

"Bare hands."

Little Bear held his hands out, fingers spread. They were large hands.

"We fight for the squaw with bare hands."

"Yes."

"She goes with the winner?"

"Yes."

"Clint—"

"Shhh."

"And if you win," Little Bear said, "you will not kill my braves?"

"No," Clint said.

"And the man in the window?" Little Bear asked. "The Salish?"

So they had been watching, which meant they had to know about Eclipse. Why would these Crow braves not want a horse like the Darley Arabian? Maybe because he was so much larger than an Indian pony.

"He won't kill anyone."

Little Bear stared at Clint, then nodded.

"And your people," Clint said, "won't kill anyone if I win?"

"They will not," Little Bear said. "They will turn, and go."

"All right, then," Clint said. "Let me go inside and tell him."

"Make him come out too and watch," Little Bear said. "I want him, and the woman, to watch."

"Sure," Clint said. "They'll watch. Let me go get him."

He would have handed Zelda his rifle, except he was afraid she would start shooting. He took it with him to the door, and opened it.

"Come on out, Ben."

The Salish came through the door, holding the rifle.

"Did you hear all that?"

"Yes."

"You won't kill anyone if I lose."

"No."

"All right. Just stand with Zelda until it's over."

"Yes."

Clint lowered his voice.

"If they don't go along with the deal, start shooting."

"Yes."

Clint turned.

"Zelda," Clint said, "stand with Ben."

She walked to them.

"You can't do this," she said. "Look at the size of him."

Little Bear had slid down off his horse. He stood at least six feet four.

"I think I can do it."

"But he's so young, so big, so strong."

"Clint is smarter," Ben said. "That will be the difference."

"Thanks, Ben."

Ben looked at Clint.

"His youth will be his undoing," the Salish said. "And his arrogance."

"Right," Clint said, unstrapped his gun and handed it to Zelda. "Be ready to throw this to me."

"Just the gun? Or the whole belt?" she asked.

"The whole thing."

"When."

"If anything goes wrong," Clint said, "you'll know when."

"Are you ready!" Little Bear called out.

Clint turned and looked. The other braves were still mounted. One of them was holding Little bear's lance.

"Are they going to stay mounted?" Clint asked.

"Yes."

He knew then that the four braves would not stick to the bargain when he beat Little Bear.

"Be ready," he told them. "When I beat him, Ben, Zelda will toss me my gun, and we'll start shooting."

"Yes," Ben said.

"But," Zelda said, "you made a bargain."

"They're not going to keep it," he told her, and turned to face the large Indian.

Chapter Twenty-Four

Clint stepped down off the porch.

Little Bear advanced on him, looking relaxed and confident—and yes, just as Ben said, arrogant.

He also looked young, strong, and impervious to pain. Clint knew the one thing he could not do was allow the younger man to get his arms around him. Little Bear would crush him.

But the thing about having all those muscles was the lack of speed. And that was what Clint was going to take advantage of.

As they began to circle each other, the Crow braves started calling out to Little Bear. Clint assumed they were cries of encouragement. On the other hand, Ben and Zelda watched in silence.

Little Bear had a smile on his face that disappeared after he made two attempts to rush in and grab Clint in a bear hug. Clint managed to step aside and avoid the brave. He assumed Little Bear was more accustomed to fighting with a knife.

"You've got to move faster than that, Little Bear," Clint said, deciding to taunt the man.

"If you will stand still I will kill you quickly."

"Kill me?"

"We are fighting for the squaw," Little Bear said. "We fight to the death."

Clint had been under the impression that all he had to do was knock Little Bear out. Now he was faced with a deadly Indian who intended to kill him.

He had to end this quickly.

"Okay, then," he said. "Come on."

This time when Little Bear charged him, Clint met him with a punch. It was a right, and hard enough to stop Little Bear in his tracks. But then he shook it off and came again. Clint had been in the boxing ring, both as a referee and a competitor. Those were the skills he was trying to use now. He hit Little Bear two times, causing the man to stagger back a few steps. Blood leaked from his nose. The Crow reached up to touch it, saw the red on his fingers, and his eyes blazed with anger.

He roared and came running at Clint, who tried to throw two punches, but the man ran through them this time. He barreled into Clint, knocking him back and off his feet. As he landed on his back Clint saw that Little Bear was going to come down on him with all his weight, so he quickly rolled to his left. He was able to avoid part of the impact, but Little Bear still landed on him. It drove some of the air out of Clint's lungs, but he still had to react. He got his hands between them, placed them on Little Bear's chest and pushed with all his might. That gave him some room to roll away and scramble to his feet.

Little Bear was slower, giving Clint a chance to kick him in the side, driving the air from his body. The Crow was barefoot, but Clint had his boots on, so he kicked him again and again. Then, when Little Bear looked up at him from his hands and knees Clint hit him with all his might, using his left because he was still safeguarding his gun hand.

Little Bear's eyes rolled up in his head and he fell onto his face and lay still.

"Now, Zelda!" Clint yelled.

As he turned toward her she tossed the gun belt to him. He caught it in his left hand and drew the gun with his right. As he turned to face the four mounted braves, they were bringing their bows around, and one was preparing to throw his lance.

The shot was from Ben's rifle, and the Crow with the lance was blown off his horse. The others drew back the strings on their bows, intending to send arrows into Clint, but he fired his Peacemaker three times rapidly. The first two braves dropped their bows and slid off their horses to the ground. The third went tumbling backward off his horse, and hit the ground with a sickening thud.

Then it was quiet.

"You knew all along they were gonna do that?" Zelda asked.

"I figured whether their man won or lost, yeah, they would," Clint said. "Kill me and Ben, and then take you."

"This was all for me?" she asked, in disbelief.

"You heard what Little Bear said," Clint answered. "You're a sturdy woman."

"Sturdy!" Zelda snapped.

"Don't worry," Clint went on, "they would've also taken whatever they wanted from the house, and probably Eclipse, too."

"That makes me feel a lot better about being called sturdy."

Ben had stepped off the porch and walked to the fallen Crow braves to check them.

"All dead," he said.

"So that just leaves Little Bear," Clint said, pointing to his unconscious foe.

"What do we do with him?" Ben asked.

"Are you gonna kill 'im?" Zelda asked.

"If we don't," Clint said, "he might just come back with more braves, next time."

"And what do we do with the bodies?"

"Ben and I will take them out in the buckboard and bury them someplace."

"Including him?" she asked, pointing at Little Bear.

"Including him," Ben said.

Chapter Twenty-Five

They hitched the mare up to the buckboard, drove it over to the house, and tossed the bodies into the back. It took both Ben and Clint to lift Little Bear, after they had tied his hands and feet. He came awake as they tossed him onto the wagon with the dead bodies.

"What are you doing?" he demanded.

"A burial party," Ben said.

"You cannot bury me with them," he complained. "I did not tell them to try and kill you."

"How do you know they did?" Clint asked. "How do you know we didn't just shoot them after I took care of you."

Little Bear's eyes darted about as he searched for an answer.

"Tie their ponies to the back," Clint told Ben. "We'll release them after the burial."

Ben nodded, and tied them off.

"You are a man of honor," Little Bear said. "You would not have killed them if they did not try to kill you."

"You came up with your answer a little late," Clint said.

They drove the bodies and Little Bear a few miles from Zelda's house, then stopped and dug one huge grave.

After they tossed the four dead Crow into it, they returned to the buckboard for Little Bear.

"You cannot do this," the Crow brave said, almost begging. "You are a man of honor."

"You are not," Ben said.

"He's right about one thing," Clint said. "I can't just kill him in cold blood."

"Then what would you do?" Ben asked. "You know if we let him go he will return, with more Crow, next time."

"No, no, I will not!" Little Bear swore. "I swear by my ancestors."

"Shoot him," Ben said.

"I can't," Clint said. "I've never killed an unarmed man before."

"Then throw him into the grave, and we will bury him," Ben suggested.

"Alive?" Clint asked.

"You would bury me alive?" Little Bear squawked.

"That's the same as shooting him," Clint said.

"Do you want to cut him loose?" Ben asked. "Let him go out here? It will take him some time to get back to his people."

"I guess we could do that," Clint said.

"With no pony, no weapons," Ben said, "and naked."

"No!" Little Bear said.

Clint studied the Crow brave and then said, "Why not?"

He heard a shot from behind him, and a bullet entered Little Bear's forehead. The brave fell over backwards in the buckboard.

Clint turned and looked at Ben, who was lowering the rifle.

"I saved you a decision," Ben said.

***

They threw Little Bear into the mass grave with the other braves, and buried them. After that they released all of the Indian ponies, and watched them run off.

"Will they return to the Crow camp?" Clint asked.

"If there is one."

Clint looked at Ben.

"There might only be these five," Ben said. "In that case, the ponies will just return to the wild."

"Let's hope that's the case."

Ben nodded.

"We better get back."

They got on the buckboard and Ben drove them back to Zelda's.

Chapter Twenty-Six

"Ben killed him?" Zelda asked.

"That's right."

"Were you gonna let 'im go?"

"I was trying to decide," Clint said.

"So he saved you the decision."

"That's how he explained it."

"Well," she said, "I'm glad he killed him. We didn't need him comin' back here with more braves." She reached across the table and touched Clint's hand that was holding his coffee cup. "I'm just glad it's over. I was afraid he'd kill you."

"It was like Ben said," Clint told her. "He was young and strong, but arrogant."

"And you're more than just a man with a fast gun," she commented.

"I've had a fight or two," he admitted.

"I was talkin' about your heart," she said. "Now get outta here and I'll make some supper."

"How are you doing on supplies?" Clint asked. "You've been using a lot since Ben and I came along."

"I always stock up, and I got the chickens out back, and got some stock to butcher. We're in good shape."

"Okay, then," Clint said. "I'm going to take Eclipse for a walk."

"Not too long a walk," Zelda said.

"Just want to stretch his legs a little," Clint said, "see how he's favoring that injured one."

"When you come in, supper will be ready."

Clint left the house, feeling that he might be getting too used to having Zelda's cooking.

When he got to the barn, Ben had already put a bridle on Eclipse and walked him out of his stall.

"How did you know?" Clint asked.

"It is time."

"Let's walk him together."

Ben nodded.

Clint took the reins and led Eclipse outside. In the beginning the Darley favored the injured leg, but the more steps he took, the more assured he became. After ten minutes he was walking well. Clint was very pleased, but he knew the horse was not ready to be ridden.

Ben walked alongside with his rifle—Zelda's rifle, actually—keeping a sharp eye out for more Crow, or the Wheelers, or anyone else who might come along.

They put Eclipse back in his stall and removed the bridle.

"Supper," Clint said.

"Good," Ben said.

They walked to the house and entered. Ben took another look at the horizon before closing the door.

"You're in time," Zelda said. "Clean your hands and sit down."

They took turns washing and then sat.

"How's your horse?" she asked Clint.

"He's good. He's walking well."

"But not ready to be ridden," she said, placing plates of steak on the table. "Not by a long shot."

"No," Clint said. "Not yet."

"Good," she said. "Don't get me wrong. I want Eclipse to heal. But I don't want you to leave yet."

"I know."

"The Wheelers," Ben said.

Clint looked at him.

"Yes, the Wheelers," he said to Ben. "We have to make sure they don't bother her."

"We can kill them," Ben said, "and dig another big grave."

"First," Clint said, "I'll try to do something without killing."

Ben shrugged and kept eating. Clint had been surprised from the beginning that the Salish knew how to use a knife and a fork.

"You think Kent Wheeler is gonna listen to reason?" Zelda asked.

"Maybe," Clint said. "Or maybe his wife will. Which of them do you know better?"

"I knew Kent before he married her," she said. "I knew his first wife, Georgia."

"How did she die?"

"A fever," she said. "Nobody's sure exactly what it was."

"And when he married Hattie and brought her back here you met her?"

"Yes," Zelda said. "I liked her, at first."

"And did she like you?"

"I think so."

"What happened?"

"Who knows?" Zelda shrugged. "One day she just wouldn't talk to me anymore."

"Maybe she thought you were sleeping with her husband?" he asked.

"Oh, no," she said. "You've seen Hattie. She was a beautiful girl when she first came here ten years ago. She's still . . ." She groped for a word.

"Handsome?"

"Yeah," Zelda said, "that's a good word."

"And how does she get along with the boys?"

"They never liked her," Zelda said. "I don't think that's changed the older they get."

"What about Wheeler?" Clint asked. "How does he get along with her?"

"He thinks he controls her," Zelda said.

"And what's the truth?"

"She wears the pants in that family."

"You know," he said. "I got that feeling. I mean, she acted like Kent was in charge. Made him think he was, even. But I got the feeling it was an act."

"Oh, it was," Zelda said. "Kent may tell his boys what to do, but it's Hattie who tells him."

"So it's Hattie who wants to buy your place?"

"I musta done somethin' to her I can't remember," Zelda said, "but I'd say yeah, she's sending her boys over here to harass me into sellin'."

"I'm sure Wheeler wouldn't tell me he wanted to buy this place just because his wife told him to," Clint said.

"Well," Zelda said "whatever the reason is, I ain't about to sell."

"Not at any price?" Clint asked.

"Not at any price."

Chapter Twenty-Seven

For the next two days Clint and Ben took turns exercising Eclipse and standing watch. Then they all ate supper together, prepared each night by Zelda. The only thing Clint and Zelda did without Ben was have sex.

On their sixth morning Zelda had made steak-and-eggs. Clint and Ben were concentrating on that when the Salish suddenly lifted his head and spoke.

"Someone is coming," he said.

Clint looked out the window, saw the rider approaching at a slow pace.

"Who is it?" Zelda asked. From her seat she could not see out the door.

"Wait," Clint said.

After a few moments there was a knock.

"I'll get it," Clint said. They had been waiting for the Wheelers to put in another appearance, but not this way.

He opened the door, saw Hattie Wheeler standing there, smiling.

"Hello, Mr. Adams."

"Mrs. Wheeler."

"Somethin' smells good. Is Zelda cookin'?"

Zelda came up and stood behind Clint.

"What are ya doin' here, Hattie?"

"Hi, Zelda," Hattie said. "It's been a while."

"Yeah, it has. Whataya want?"

"I wanna talk to Mr. Adams," Hattie said. She looked at Clint. "Can we go for a walk?"

"Sure," Clint said. "Why not?"

Hattie leaned over to look at Zelda.

"Can I borrow him?" she asked.

"As long as you bring him back."

"Oh," Hattie said, "I will." She looked at Clint. "Should we go?"

Since Clint already had his gun on his hip, all he needed to do was grab his hat.

"Let's go."

He stepped outside, looked around to make sure the other Wheelers weren't with her, then looked at Hattie.

"Mr. Adams?" She smiled that pretty smile. "I didn't suppose you wanted Zelda to hear that we were friendly," she said. "Let's walk."

They stepped off the porch and started to walk slowly. He was heading for the barn, but she subtly steered him away from it.

"What's on your mind, Hattie?" he asked.

"You mean besides bein' on my kitchen table with you?" she asked.

"Yes, I mean besides that."

"Look, Clint," she said, "what are the chances that Zelda will sell us her place?"

"I'd say no chance at all."

"Really?" Hattie asked. "Not for any amount of money?"

"Why?" Clint asked. "How much money do you have?"

"A lot," she said, laughing.

"Then why do you need this place?"

"The money," she said, "is to buy this place." He turned them toward the barn, again.

"So somebody gave you the money to buy Zelda's ranch?" he asked. "Why?"

She stopped walking.

"I never said that."

"You did," he said. "Kind of."

"Look," she said, "I just came here to see what you could tell me—"

"Wait," he said.

"What?"

"Every time I head for the barn, you steer us away," he said.

"What are you talkin'—"

He turned and ran for the barn.

Chapter Twenty-Eight

"Wait—" she shouted, but he kept running.

As he entered the barn, he saw Dave and Leonard trying to remove Eclipse from his stall, but the Darley was resisting their efforts.

"You know," Clint said, "I should let you keep trying. You're just going to lose some fingers."

The two Wheeler boys turned toward him, then looked at their rifles, which were leaning against the stall.

"Don't even think about it," he said.

They looked from their rifles to Clint and back again, releasing their hold on Eclipse's mane. One of them was holding the bridle, which they had obviously meant to put on him.

"Listen to him, boys," Hattie said, from the door. "Don't go for those guns. He'd kill you both. Just wait outside. I'll be right there."

"Can we take our rifles?" Leonard asked,

"No," Clint said, "just go."

"Do as he says," Hattie told them.

They both moved past Clint and Hattie and walked outside.

"I'm sorry—"

"Where's your husband?" he asked.

"I didn't include him in this," she said. "I thought the boys could handle it."

"Did you really?" he asked. "This was your idea, to steal my horse?"

"I just thought you cared more about the horse than you did about Zelda," she said, "and that if we had him, you'd work with us."

"You thought wrong," he said. "I'm not going to work with you, so you better go."

"Can I take their rifles?"

"No."

"Okay," Hattie said. "But this ain't over. Tell Zelda she should sell, for her own good."

"And what's that mean?"

"Just tell 'er," she said. "And you and me? We ain't done, either."

She turned and walked out into the sun, which made her simple cotton dress seem transparent.

Clint walked to Eclipse, who stuck his big head out of the stall.

"It's okay, boy," he said, stroking his neck. "I know if you were feeling yourself you would've taken care of those two yahoos."

Eclipse tossed his head, as if to say, "You're so right."

"I'm not feeling tip-top myself, yet," Clint said. "Maybe in a few days . . . And don't worry. Ben or me will be in here with you all the time, from now on."

He returned to the house, sent Ben right out to the barn to sit with Eclipse. Ben grabbed Zelda's rifle and took it with him.

"What did Hattie have to say?" Zelda asked. "Did she try to get your pants off in the barn?"

"That would have been embarrassing," Clint said, "since her sons were out there."

Her eyes widened.

"What were they—did they try to hurt Eclipse?"

"No," Clint said, "just tried to kidnap him."

"And luckily you stopped them."

"Yes."

"Without a shot," she added, "so I guess you didn't kill 'em."

"I don't ever kill unless I have to," he said.

She had witnessed that, with his reluctance to kill the Crow brave, Little Bear.

"So now what?" she asked.

"I went to talk to Kent Wheeler, and then the Wheelers came here to steal my horse," he said. "But they left Kent out."

"I told you," Zelda said, "Hattie runs things."

"Well, maybe if I approach Kent with that, he'll turn around and bite her in the britches—so to speak."

"Play them against each other?"

"Why not?"

"You know," she said, "Kent's always been the kind of man a woman could control. How do you plan to change him?"

"By challenging him," Clint said.

"How do you challenge a man who can't control his own woman?" she asked.

"Did your husband control you?"

"We was a team," she said. "That was different."

"Well, I think you can challenge any man if you bruise his ego."

"Do me a favor," she said. "While yer bruisin' his ego, put a few bruises on his butt for me."

"Does wheeler go to Halsey for supplies?" Clint asked.

"Just like me, he's got to. It's the closest place."

"They got a saloon?"

"Kinda," she said. "It's in the trading post."

"Okay," Clint said, "so I get him to meet me there, get him liquored up, and start bruising."

"How you gonna get him to go?"

"I'll send Ben with a message."

"Better hope they don't shoot him on sight."

Clint smiled.

"You can't shoot what you can't see."

Chapter Twenty-Nine

Clint wrote the message out and gave it to Ben to deliver. He told the Salish to leave Zelda's rifle.

"But don't let anybody see you."

Ben grinned and left.

"What will you do now?" Zelda asked.

"Saddle your mare and head for Halsey."

"I'll get dressed and we'll hitch the mare to the buckboard—" she started.

"We can't do that, Zelda," Clint said.

"Why not?"

"I need somebody here to watch over Eclipse. That's why I had Ben leave your rifle. I can't be sure Wheeler will come to Halsey. If he thinks I'm there, he might come here."

"And if he does?"

"Ben should be back by then."

"But if he shows up—"

"Do what you have to."

"I can shoot him?"

"If it comes to that."

She smiled.

Clint saddled the mare once again, and rode out, following Zelda's directions. He hoped Ben would succeed in delivering the message. He probably should have waited for word that he had, but he wanted to get to Halsey before Kent Wheeler did. He couldn't trust that he'd be able to do that on Zelda's mare unless he left right away. Hopefully, he wasn't making a mistake, but he thought his message to Wheeler would be irresistible. It read: YOUR WIFE AND BOYS CAME TO SEE ME TODAY. WANT TO KNOW WHAT THEY SAID? LET'S HAVE A DRINK IN HALSEY.

He thought that would do it.

***

Zelda had been right. Halsey wasn't much. In fact, he was surprised it had a name. She also told him there was no lawman. That wasn't a surprise. As he rode in, it was late afternoon, since it had taken him hours to get there on the mare, even though he had pushed her.

He saw a couple of buildings that looked as if they were about to fall down. Then there was the trading post, and a barn with an empty corral. He assumed that would be the livery, but he reined in the mare right in front of the trading post and dismounted. There were two other horses there. He hoped one wasn't Kent Wheeler's.

Neither horse had been there long enough for the sweat to dry on their coats, which meant they had been ridden in within the past few minutes.

Inside there was one man standing at a makeshift bar that looked as if it had been constructed from an old door, and another was walking around, looking at items on shelves and in barrels. The second man stuck his hand in one barrel and came out with a pickle.

"You're gonna hafta pay for that!" the man behind the bar shouted.

"Take it easy," the man standing at the bar said. "Just give us two beers. We'll pay."

The man behind the bar was a barrel-chested fifty or so. He had a sour look on his face that Clint felt was probably always there.

The second man continued to walk around, eating the pickle. He and the man at the bar wore dust-covered trail clothes, and guns on their hips.

Clint walked to the bar. The bartender looked at him.

"Got any beer?" Clint asked.

"That's what I'm givin' them," the bartender said.

"I'll have one, too."

"Us first," the man with the pickle said, coming over to the bar. "We were here first."

"Relax," Clint said. "It doesn't matter who was here first. I'll buy."

"You heard the man!" the first one said.

"Does that include the pickle?" the second one asked.

"Sure," Clint said, "pickle included."

"Thanks, friend!"

***

Clint had a second beer with the two men. He was wondering if there was going to be trouble, but eventually they thanked him and left.

"I wanna thank ya," the bartender said.

"What for?"

"I had a feelin' I was gonna have trouble with those two," he said. "In fact, I thought they wuz gonna rob me. And they might've, if you hadn't come along when you did."

"No problem," Clint said. "I'm waiting to meet some-body here, so I'll have another one."

"Sure, friend," the bartender said, "on the house this time, okay?"

"Okay with me."

The bartender gave him another lukewarm beer.

"I got some whiskey here if you'd rather have it," he said.

"No, this is fine."

"I know it ain't cold."

"It's wet," Clint said. "That'll be good enough, for now."

Chapter Thirty

"Ain't seen you around here before," the bartender said.

"That's because I've never been here before."

"So what brings ya here now?"

"Like I said," Clint answered. "I'm meeting somebody. Maybe you know him? Kent Wheeler?"

"Wheeler, yeah," the man said. "He buys his supplies here. Hey, you want a pickle?"

"No, thanks. What's your name?"

"Farley," the man said.

"Well, Mr. Farley—"

"Just Farley."

"Okay, Farley," Clint said. "What do you know about Wheeler?"

"He's got two sons, and a wife he complains about," Farley said. "But who doesn't, right? My old lady gives me hell every day. But I still love 'er."

"I'm sure you do," Clint said.

"You got business with Wheeler?"

"I don't know," Clint said. "I guess that depends on how things go. Why? Should I be warned about something?"

"I'd warn you about his wife," Farley said, "not him."

"Does she come here to shop?"

"Not as much as him, but she's been here."

"With or without him?"

"Oh, without," he said. "She wouldn't be able to get up to some of the things she does if he was here."

"Other men?"

"Oh, yeah."

"Have you ever told him?"

"No, no," Farley said. "I stay outta other people's business—especially other people's marriages."

"How do you think he'd react if somebody told him?" Clint asked.

"You know," Farley said, "I find it kinda hard to believe he don't already know. I mean, she ain't exactly secretive about it, ya know?"

"I think I do."

Clint heard a horse approaching. If it was two he might have thought the other two men were leaving, but this was one horse, so he guessed it was being ridden in.

Then a man came through the door and looked around.

"Speak of the devil," Farley muttered, and moved away.

Wheeler saw Clint and came over.

"Farley," he called out, "gimme one of them godawful warm beers of yers."

"Comin' up, Mr. Wheeler."

As Farley put the beer down on the bar, Wheeler asked Clint, "This on you?"

"It is."

Wheeler picked up the mug and drained it, then waved it at Farley, who brought another.

"Okay," Wheeler said. "I'm here. How much ya want?"

"What do you mean?"

"I figure yer wantin' to sell yer services," Wheeler said. "Make some money fer gettin' Zelda to sell."

"I'm here to talk about your wife and sons."

"I thought that note was just ta get me here," Wheeler said.

"They came to Zelda's ranch and tried to steal my horse," Clint told him.

"What? When?"

"This morning."

"Sonofabitch. I wondered where they went!" he growled. "I didn't send 'em. I ain't all right with stealin' a man's horse."

"Well, your wife kept me busy outside while your boys tried to grab him," Clint said. "I stopped them without killing anyone, but next time—"

"Ain't gonna be no next time," Wheeler said, cutting him off.

"So you're giving up on trying to buy the place?"

"No," he said, "I ain't, but nobody's gonna try ta steal yer horse again. Ya got my word on that."

Clint found himself believing the man.

"Now let's talk business," Wheeler said.

"Okay," Clint said. "Your wife told me you've got a lot of money to spend. Who gave it to you?"

"Whataya mean? It's mine."

"Come on, Wheeler," Clint said. "Somebody's paying you to make these offers."

"Whataya talkin' about?"

"I'm saying I don't think you have the money to do this on your own," Clint said. "Somebody put you up to it."

"Who?"

The man looked legitimately puzzled. Clint was starting to wonder if Hattie was in complete control of this situation. Maybe somebody was paying *her*, but her husband and sons didn't know it.

Maybe he could play them against each other.

"What about your wife?"

"What about her?" He looked even more puzzled by the question.

"Could somebody be paying her?"

"For what? I don't know what yer talkin' about."

"Maybe you better ask her, then," Clint said. "Maybe she knows what's going on."

Wheeler frowned.

"Yer tryin' ta confuse me," he said, finally. He turned around and left.

Clint didn't think he had to try all that hard.

Chapter Thirty-One

Clint knew if he headed back to Zelda's he would get there after dark, but he had no choice. There was no hotel in Halsey, and he didn't feel safe staying away from Zelda's overnight.

He thought about buying some supplies, but he didn't know if Zelda needed anything. She had assured him they had plenty. In the end he just bought coffee, and some bullets, then went out to his mare.

As he put the coffee and bullets in his saddlebags, he saw that the other two horses were still there. Wheeler had already mounted and left. He had heard the horse gallop.

If these two horses were still here where were the riders?

Farley had said he thought they were going to rob him. Maybe they were waiting for Clint to leave. Could he ride out without finding out for sure?

He mounted the mare and rode out.

***

Farley looked at the door as the two cowboys came back in.

"Now we can finish our business," the one who had eaten the pickle said.

"What business?" Farley asked. "Your pickle was paid for."

The second man pulled his gun and pointed it at the bartender.

"Bring both hands out where I can see them," he said, "and one of them better not be holding a shotgun."

Farley took his hand off the shotgun under the bar and raised his hands.

"I knew you guys were trouble."

"Just put the money on the bar and there won't be any," the pickle man said.

"I don't have any money," Farley said. "You guys and that other one were my only customers today."

"You better not be tellin' the truth," the man with the gun said. He looked at the pickle man. "Check it."

The pickle man nodded, walked around behind the bar. First, he brought the shotgun out and then a metal cashbox.

"Oh yeah," he told his partner. "Plenty of cash in here."

"Take it!"

The pickle man put his hand in the box, and that's when Clint came back through the door.

"Don't do it," he said.

***

Clint had ridden just far enough out of town that the walk back wouldn't be too long. Then he tied the mare to a bush and took the walk. As he approached the trading post he heard the voices inside.

". . . plenty of cash in here."

"Take it!"

He stepped inside.

"Don't do it."

He saw one man holding a gun, and the pickle man was behind the bar with Farley, a shotgun and a cash box.

"What're you doin' here?" the pickle man asked.

"Keeping you from robbing this store," Clint said. "You with the gun. Drop it."

He was behind the man, so there was no way for the gunman to know if Clint had his gun out or not.

"Jed?" he said.

"His gun's in his holster, Dack."

"And so's yours," Clint said to Jed.

"You never shoulda come back," Jed said. "Kill 'im, Dack."

As the man started to turn, Clint drew, and as Dack came around with his gun he shot him in the chest.

Instead of going for his holstered weapon, Jed picked the shotgun up off the bar.

"Don't be stupid!" Clint shouted.

He continued to bring the shotgun up, as Clint shot him, also in the chest. He dropped behind the bar.

"Farley!"

"He's dead, he's dead," Farley said. "Don't shoot!"

"Okay, get out from behind there," Clint said.

Farley obeyed.

Clint checked on Dack, found him dead, then went behind the bar and checked Jed. Also dead. He picked up the shotgun, put it on top of the bar. He replaced the spent shells in his gun with live ammo, and holstered it.

"Okay," Clint said, "I understand you have no law here?"

"No," Farley said, "we're not really a town."

"Can you deal with these two?"

"Huh? Oh, sure. Yeah, I can get rid of 'em."

"Then do it," Clint said. "I've got to go."

"Okay," Farley said, "but . . . thanks."

"Sure."

Clint started out.

"Hey, Mister!"

Clint turned.

"Watch out for them Wheelers," Farley said. "They're crazy."

"Which one?" Clint asked.

"All of 'em."

Chapter Thirty-Two

Wheeler rode hard and got back home before dark. He left his horse out front and stormed into the house.

"Kent!" Hattie said. "Where've you—"

"You boys go out and take care of my horse!" he barked.

They were sitting at the table, with plates of food in front of them.

"We're eatin', Pa," Dave said.

"You can finish eatin' after you take care of my horse," Kent called. "Now move!"

Dave jerked his head at his brother. They both stood and went outside.

"What's goin' on?" Hattie asked.

"Suppose you tell me that," Kent said.

"Whataya mean?"

"I mean," Kent said, "why do we all of a sudden have so much money to buy Zelda's ranch?"

"I told you," she said. "It was left to me by a relative back East—"

"Yeah," he said, "I know you *told* me that."

"And now you don't believe me?" she asked. "Where did you just go? Who did you see?"

"I went to Halsey," Kent said, "and I saw the Gun-smith."

She folded her arms.

"And what did he tell you?"

"That you took the boys over there and tried to kidnap his horse," Kent said. "A man's horse, Hattie?"

"Oh, don't give me that crap about a man and his horse," she said, in disgust.

Wheeler charged and grabbed her by the throat with one powerful hand. Her eyes bugged out.

"Kent—" she choked out.

"Nobody touches that horse again," he said. "Do you understand?"

"I can't—"

"Just nod if you understand."

She nodded jerkily.

"All right." He released his hold on her throat. "Now tell me about the money."

***

It was getting dark when Clint rode the exhausted mare up to Zelda's barn. He dismounted and walked her inside. He found himself looking down the barrel of a rifle in Ben's hands.

"It's me," Clint said.

Ben lowered the rifle.

"She looks bad," Ben said, about the mare.

"I know," Clint said. "I pushed. I better get this saddle off of her."

While he unsaddled the mare, Ben asked, "Did you see Wheeler?"

"Yeah, he didn't know anything about his wife and boys trying to grab Eclipse. In fact, he was mad when I told him."

"Angry?"

"Oh yeah," Clint said. "He said I shouldn't worry about anybody trying to kidnap Eclipse again."

"And you believed him?"

"I did," Clint said, "but that doesn't mean he's not dangerous. In fact, according to a bartender in Halsey, the whole family is crazy."

He finished unsaddling the mare, rubbed her down and gave her some feed. She was blowing hard, and he hoped she would catch her breath and make it through the night.

"I didn't accomplish anything solid," he told Ben, "but I might have turned them against each other. Only time will tell."

"You can go inside and talk to Zelda," Ben said. "I will stay here."

"Okay," Clint said. "I'll see you in a while."

Ben nodded. Clint grabbed the saddlebags from the mare's saddle and carried them to the house with him.

***

Zelda was starting to worry about Clint as it got dark, but then saw him ride up to the barn. She and Ben had not waited for him to eat, so she quickly doled out a portion of beef stew in a bowl and had it on the table when he walked in.

"Thought you'd be hungry," she said.

"Thanks. I bought some more coffee while I was there."

"Oh, thanks." She took the coffee from the saddlebags, set the bullets aside, and hung the bags from a peg on the wall.

As Clint sat and started to eat, she brought him a cup of coffee.

"How did it go?" she asked. "Whatever you did?"

"I saw Kent Wheeler," he said, and told her how angry he had gotten when told about his boys trying to kidnap Eclipse.

"Well," she said, "he's a rancher, after all. And a man. You of all people know how men are with their horses."

"Yes I do," he said.

"What else happened?"

"I planted a seed," he said. "Hopefully, he and his wife will start bickering."

"They're husband and wife," she said. "They do that, anyway."

"And I stopped two men from robbing the trading post."

"I'll bet Farley liked that."

"He did," Clint said, "but I left him to clean up the mess."

"You killed 'em?"

"They didn't give me a choice."

"Farley'll get rid of them."

"Yeah, he seemed like a good man."

"He is."

She sat across from him.

"I gotta thank you for stayin' around here this long," she said.

"Well, I've got to wait for Eclipse to be ready for me to ride."

"Yeah but I think you woulda been gone by now if you hadn't got mixed up with the Wheelers. I can handle 'em, ya know. You don't have to stay."

"I'll see it out, Zelda," he said. "Besides, where else am I going to find food this good?"

Chapter Thirty-Three

Clint went out to the barn a couple of hours later, handed Ben one of the cups of coffee he was carrying.

"Why don't you go and get some sleep, Ben," he said. "I'll watch Eclipse."

"I can sleep out here," Ben said. "You should go and be with Zelda."

Clint studied the Salish's face, not sure how he meant that. Did he know that he and Zelda were sharing her bed?

"All right," he said, "but I'll stay out here a while. How's the mare?"

"Her breathing is back to normal," Ben said. "She will be fine, if she gets some rest."

"We'll have to try not to use her for a while," Clint commented.

"How much longer will you be staying here?" Ben asked.

"I don't know," Clint said. "Until I get the Wheelers off Zelda's back, I guess. But you don't have to stay, Ben. You must've been on your way somewhere when you found me and Eclipse out there."

"No," Ben said. "My people put me out, and I was . . . wandering. I am happy to stay with you and Zelda until the end."

"All right, then," Clint said. "I'll check in on you and the horses in a few hours."

Ben nodded. Clint left the barn and headed back to the house.

***

Kent Wheeler waited for his boys to come into the barn.

"Close the doors," he instructed them.

Each boy took an oversized door and closed it.

"Lock it!" Kent ordered.

"Who we lockin' out, Pa?" Dave asked as Leonard locked the doors. "Adams?"

"Your mother."

"Ma?" Dave said. "But—"

Kent pointed to two bales of hay and said, "Sit, both of you."

They sat and waited.

"From now on," Kent said, "you two will be doin' what I say, not what your mother says. Understand?"

"But . . . Ma says—" Leonard started, only to be cut off angrily by his father.

"I don't care what your mother says! She can't whip your asses the way I can."

The two boys looked at each other. Lately, they had been talking about which one of them could whip their Pa's ass, if it came to that. Dave was older, but Leonard was slightly larger.

"Don't even think about it," Kent said. "I can still whip either one of you."

"But . . ." Dave said.

"But what?" Kent asked. "Not at the same time. Is that what your mother wants from you? For the two of you to go against me?"

"She's not our mother, Pa," Dave said. "She's our step-mother."

"Well, your step-mother is makin' decisions she shouldn't be makin'."

"Like what?" Leonard asked, genuinely interested.

"Like tryin' to steal the Gunsmith's horse," Kent said. "You don't steal a man's horse. A man don't do that."

"Okay, Pa," Dave said. "We won't do it."

"So what do we tell Hattie?" Leonard asked.

"When she tells you to do somethin'," Kent said, "you check with me first. Got it?"

"We got it, Pa," Dave assured him.

"Good. You can go now."

"That's it?" Dave asked.

"That's it."

He exchanged glances with his younger brother, and then they unlocked the door and left the barn.

Kent Wheeler stayed behind, because he still had some decisions to make.

Chapter Thirty-Four

As had become his routine, Clint slipped out of bed without waking Zelda. Wearing her out during the night made it easier. His own legs felt weak as he dressed, but he managed to strap on his gun and leave the bedroom without falling down.

He poured two cups of coffee from the pot on the pot-bellied stove and carried them out to the barn. Ben looked at him as he walked in, and he wondered if the old Salish ever slept.

"Thank you," Ben said, accepting it. "Coffee is one of the things the white man has done right."

"No argument from me, there," Clint agreed.

"I was wondering . . ." Ben started.

"About what?"

"Would not it make sense to solve Zelda's problems with the Wheelers by . . . killing them?"

Clint answered without hesitation.

"I suppose it would, if I was that kind of man."

"But you are not?"

"No," Clint said. "I'm afraid if I was, I wouldn't like myself very much."

Ben nodded and sipped his coffee.

"You're not thinking about doing something like that, are you?" Clint asked.

"No," Ben said. "I will do as you ask."

"Good. Did you sleep at all last night?"

"Some."

"You want me to take over here?"

"I am fine," Ben said. "I like being with the horses."

"Have you heard anything else to indicate there might be someone out there?"

"No, nothing," Ben said. "And the Wheelers would not be able to hide the sound of their shod horses from me."

"I believe you."

"So are we still going to just . . . wait?"

"Yes," Clint said. "I want to see if I accomplished anything by talking to Kent Wheeler yesterday. But whether I did or not, they're going to have to make another move soon."

"You think someone is directing them?"

"That's exactly what I think," Clint said.

"Who could be doing that?"

"Somebody who has plans for all this property, is my guess," Clint said. "That's why they've got Wheeler trying to buy it. And they've probably already bought Wheeler's place."

"But the ranches are so far apart," Ben pointed out.

"Which means it must be something big."

Ben shook his head.

"White men."

"I know," Clint said. "Indians are much more obvious about the things they want."

"White men are . . . confusing."

"I can understand why you'd feel that way."

"But not you."

"No, not me."

"I have heard of you," Ben said. "The Salish know your reputation."

"Is that why you helped me?"

"I helped you because you and your horse needed it," Ben said. "Then I found out who you were."

"Well, I'm glad you're here."

"You should go to the house," Ben said, "I will stay here and make sure nothing happens to your horses."

"I appreciate that," Clint said. "I'll see you later, for breakfast."

Clint left the barn and went back to the house.

***

"Will Ben be comin' for breakfast?" Zelda asked, getting out of the bedroom as Clint entered.

"Yes."

"I'll get it goin', then."

Clint sat at the kitchen table.

"More coffee?" she asked.

"Please."

She took his cup, filled it and brought it back to him, then put her hand on his shoulder.

"When this is over you'll leave, won't you?" she asked.

"Yes."

"I'll miss you," she said, "but you've given me somethin' I've been missin' for a long time."

He smiled and asked, "Sex?"

She laughed.

"That, too," she said, "but I just mean a connection, and a reason to believe that maybe my life's not over."

"Your life is far from over, Zelda."

"I wasn't believin' that," she said. "Now I do. There might even be room for another man in my life."

"I hope so," Clint said. "You deserve to be happy."

"We just need to handle the Wheelers," she said, walking to the stove.

"And we will," Clint said. "Hopefully, they're handling each other right now."

Chapter Thirty-Five

Over breakfast Clint explained to Zelda and Ben what he hoped was happening right at that moment.

"So you think you might've started them fightin' among themselves?" she asked.

"That's what I'm hoping."

"What makes you think they'll do that?" she asked.

"She came here with her boys to try to steal my horse," he said. "Kent Wheeler wasn't in on that."

"Are you sure?" Zelda asked.

"He was angry when I told him what they did," Clint said. "It was real."

"But maybe it was because they didn't get the horse," she suggested.

"No," Clint said, "he didn't know what they were doing, and he didn't like it when he realized the truth. I'm pretty sure of that."

"So now what?"

"They'll make a move, soon," Clint said. "Unless they battle amongst themselves, and something happens."

"Like what?" Zelda asked. When Clint didn't answer she asked, "Do you think Kent might kill Hattie?"

"Or maybe the other way around," Clint said, "because they sure as hell don't seem to be working together."

"And the boys?" she asked. "They're just a couple of stupid kids."

"They're not kids," Clint said, "they're men. And they're probably a little confused about who they should be listening to."

"Hattie," Zelda said.

"You think so?"

"She'll take control," Zelda said. "Of the boys, and of Kent. You probably started some trouble, but she'll take control."

"I'm not sure I want that," Clint said.

"Does it make a difference?" she asked.

"Maybe not," Clint said. "I just think I can get to Kent better than I can get to Hattie."

"You're probably right," Zelda said. "Unless you let her get to you."

"What do you mean?"

"I mean she's a slut," Zelda said, "and an ex-whore. But I don't think she's ever been with a man like you. Maybe you can use that."

"Are you telling me to sleep with her to win her over to my side?"

"I'm sure you'd do whatever you had to do to save your horse."

"Or you."

"That's sweet," she said, "but I don't want you to poke her to save me."

They both looked at Ben to see if he had any idea what they were talking about. If he did, he just stared off and pretended not to.

***

The two boys, Dave and Leonard, were in the house with Hattie, while Kent stayed outside.

"What did he want?" she asked them.

"He told us to do what he says, not what you say," Leonard answered.

"And you told him you would?"

"Yes."

"That's good."

"But . . ." Dave started.

"But what?"

"We ain't gonna do nothin' to hurt our Pa," Dave said.

"I don't want you to hurt him," she said. "I just want you to do what I say."

"So does he," Leonard said.

"Yeah," she said, opening the top of her shirt, "but he's not gonna give you these, is he?" She held her bare breasts in her hands, and thumbed the nipples hard.

"Jesus," Leonard said, licking his lips.

"No," Dave said, staring, "he ain't."

***

"I just thought of something," Clint said, as Ben left the house to go back to the barn.

"What?" Zelda asked, cleaning the plates off the table.

"Would Hattie use sex on those boys?"

She stopped and looked at him.

"I'm sure she would," she said. "After all, they're not her sons."

"That's right, they're not," he said.

"But . . . you said she came here ten years ago."

"She did."

"So she's been raising them since then?"

"If you're thinkin' that she's had any motherly feelin's for them boys, take my word for it. She ain't. Hattie ain't the mother type."

"Okay," he said, "if she's going to use sex to get them on her side, then she's going to get her way."

"Yeah, she is."

"That poor sap," Clint said, thinking about Wheeler.

"Yeah he is," she said, and continued to clean up.

159

Chapter Thirty-Six

"You want us to what?" Dave asked.

"Kill Zelda," Hattie said.

"Why?" Leonard asked.

"I don't want you to be askin' me why," she told them. "Just do it!"

"What about the Gunsmith?" Dave asked. "He ain't just gonna let us."

"Then kill him, too."

"Just us?" Leonard asked.

"You got anybody else in mind to help you?" Hattie asked.

Leonard looked at Dave.

"We can get some boys to back us up," Dave assured her, even though his brother was frowning at him.

"Good," Hattie said. "Then do it. In fact, you know what?" She was getting excited. "Kill everyone there and burn the place to the ground."

"Hattie—" Dave said.

"Leonard, go outside and let me know if your father's comin'," Hattie said.

"Yes, "Ma'am."

As the door closed Dave turned to look at Hattie. She had already dropped her dress to the ground. Hungrily, his eyes scanned her naked body, stopping first at her breasts, and then at the dark tangle of hair between her thighs.

"Well, come on," she said, waving him over, "but we gotta be quick."

He crossed the room quickly, already unbuttoning his trousers. As he reached her, she fell to her knees and pulled out his young cock. It was longer and prettier than his father's, and she quickly took it into her mouth. She had been promising both boys sex as a reward for the longest time, but what Lenny didn't know was that she had already given it to Dave a few times.

"Oh God!" Dave muttered, trying to keep quiet so his brother wouldn't hear. But Hattie was an expert cock-sucker, and she brought him up onto his toes before she let him slide wetly from her mouth.

"Okay, you're good and hard, lover," she said. "Shove it in."

She hitched herself up onto the edge of the stove so he could drive it into her and start pumping his hips franti-cally . . .

***

When the front door opened Leonard turned and watched his brother come out. He was still fixing his pants.

"What'd you do?"

Dave didn't answer.

"You poked 'er, didn't ya?" Leonard asked. "God-damn! You did it."

"You'll get your chance," Dave said. "Right now we got work ta do."

The two boys stepped down off the steps.

"You poked 'er," Leonard said. again. "Was she good, brother?"

"Mighty good!" Dave said, with a smile. "And she couldn't get enough."

"Jesus."

"Never mind," Dave said. "Hattie wants us ta do somethin', and we gotta do it."

"Yeah, but what do we tell Pa?"

"I'll think of somethin'," Dave said.

***

Kent Wheeler wondered if he was going to have to kill his wife? Even after ten years together, he still didn't understand the woman. And rather than try, maybe he should just get rid of her. He didn't know what she'd been thinking when she told his boys to steal the Gunsmith's horse. She could've got them killed.

He decided it was time to go to the house and deal with her.

***

Hattie put her dress back on and looked out the window. Dave had stuck his dick in her and lasted a whole two minutes. She doubted Leonard would last that long. It was going to be easy to keep those boys in line. Maybe she could even train them to satisfy her. Young dicks were better than old ones any day of the week. All she had to do was teach them to last longer when they were poking her.

She was tired of her husband in more ways than one, but the sex had been bad from the beginning. His dick was a huge, ugly veiny thing. Dave's was long and smooth, and she figured Lenny's would be the same.

She just had to convince them each that they were the only one for her.

***

The boys disappeared behind the barn just as Kent came out of it. He started toward the house with long, purposeful strides. He had something on his mind, and he wasn't going to be as easy to control as the boys.

She walked to a kitchen drawer, opened it and took out a knife.

***

Kent Wheeler entered the house, saw Hattie standing there with her hands behind her back.

"We gotta talk," he said.

"Do we?" she asked. "I'm tired of talkin'. When are you gonna act?"

"When I'm good and damn ready, woman!" he snapped. "You don't tell me what to do, and I don't want you tellin' my boys."

"They ain't boys!" she snapped. "When are you gonna realize that and start treatin' them like men?"

"Is that what you're doin'?" he asked. "Treatin' them like men?" He came closer to her. She was determined that he was never going to put his hands around her neck, again.

"More than you," she said.

"You're supposed to be their mother!"

"I ain't never been their mother," she said, "and they ain't ever felt that way about me."

"You bitch!" he raged "whataya been doin' with my boys?"

He reached out for her neck, and she brought the knife around from behind her back.

Chapter Thirty-Seven

That evening Clint took a wooden chair out to the porch with him and sat down. After a few minutes Zelda came out with two coffee mugs.

"You know," he said. "I never thought I'd ever say this, but I'm about filled to here with coffee."

She smiled and handed him a mug.

"That's why I added a generous bit of whiskey to this one," she said.

"You've got whiskey in the house?" he asked. "Where have you been hiding it? And why?"

She sat down on the edge of the porch, almost at his feet.

"I ain't gonna tell you where it is," she said. "It's private. Besides, we got an Indian livin' with us."

"I don't think Ben is that kind of Indian," Clint told her.

"All I know is Indians ain't supposed to be able to handle fire water," she said. "So I keep it hidden."

"Well, it's your house," he said, "and your whiskey." He sipped his coffee and the whiskey burned its way down his throat.

"Where did you get this stuff?" he choked.

"From Farley, in Halsey," she said.

"Whoa, it's raw," he said, setting the mug down on the porch,

"You don't like it?"

"I'm a beer man," he said, "so you go ahead and keep that stuff hidden away, and take it out when *you* want it."

"I'm gonna turn in," she said, getting to her feet. "I know you wanna sit out here alone for a while."

"I do," he said. "I've got some thinking to do."

She went inside and left him to it.

***

After about an hour alone with his thoughts Clint got up and walked to the barn, again. Ben eyed him as he entered.

"Have you thought of something?" the Salish asked.

"I have," Clint said. "I've been thinking about what you said."

"About killing them?"

"Yes."

"I can do it, if you do not want to," Ben said.

"I'm thinking I may not have to actually kill them. They just have to think I will."

"You are going to threaten them?"

"Not the wife," Clint said. "I don't think she'd respond to threats."

"What about the husband?"

"Kent," Clint said. "I could probably do it, but he'd take longer."

"Than the sons?"

"Yes," Clint said. "I don't know if they've ever had dealings with Indians."

"You want me to frighten them?"

Clint looked at Ben. He wasn't tall, very thin, somewhere between sixty and seventy years old. Yet he did project something other than the image of a frail, old man. To the Wheeler boys, he might look pretty savage.

"I think maybe we can frighten them, together," Clint said, finally.

"But frighten them into doing what?"

"I haven't thought of that, yet," Clint said, "or how we can get to them."

"I can get to them," Ben said.

"How?"

"I will go there," the Salish said, "to their ranch."

"Maybe we should both go," Clint said. "You take care of the boys, and I'll talk to Kent and his wife."

"What about Zelda?" Ben asked. "Will she be safe here?"

"She can take care of herself until we get back," Clint said.

"And Eclipse?"

"Is the mare ready to travel?" Clint asked.

"I doubt it," Ben said. "You took a lot out of her."

"Then I'll have to risk riding Eclipse," Clint said. "If we can get to the Wheeler place before they decide to come back here, we can end this."

Chapter Thirty-Eight

They left the barn together, Clint heading back to the house, and Ben starting off on foot, carrying Clint's rifle. Moving by night he was sure that he would be at the Wheeler ranch in the morning. It was unlikely the Wheelers would be active at night. Somehow, Clint didn't think Kent Wheeler was a killer, or that the sons were, either. But Hattie, according to Zelda, was a woman who knew what she wanted, and would do anything to get it. Clint had already experienced some of that. He just didn't know if sex with Hattie Wheeler was enough to convince Dave and Leonard to become killers.

As he entered the house he looked into the bedroom, saw Zelda asleep in bed. He hated to wake her, but she had to know what he and Ben had decided to do.

He went in, sat beside her, put a hand out to rouse her gently, then explained what he and Ben had discussed.

"Ben's already on the way?" she asked. "On foot?"

"It's the way he travels," Clint said. "He'll be there by morning."

"And how will you get there?"

"I'm going to leave early on Eclipse, so I don't have to push him too hard."

"He can use the exercise," she admitted. "I think he's ready, but you're right not to push him."

"So you should get some sleep," Clint said. "You'll have to be alert tomorrow."

"Why don't I just come with you?" she asked.

"The mare's in no shape to be ridden, or to hitch to that buckboard. And Eclipse can't carry us both. No, you'll have to stay here. You'll have your rifle."

"I'll be fine," she said. "I'll just be worried about you."

"I'm fine," he said. "I think I'm finally back to normal, so it's time for me to take charge. I think we can end this tomorrow, but that means finding out who really wants to buy your ranch, and why."

"Now that's somethin' I'd really like to know," she admitted.

"Then let's get some sleep," Clint said.

He laid himself down next to Zelda, keeping his clothes on, his gun belt right at hand. He wanted to get a quick start in the morning, and not have to take time to get dressed.

***

At first light Clint woke Zelda to tell her he was leaving.

"You and Ben come back alive," she told him.

"That's the plan."

She rose to get dressed while he went out to the barn to saddle Eclipse for the first time since he was injured.

"Okay, big boy," Clint said, putting Eclipse's blanket on his back, "I can see you've lost some weight, but this exercise is going to do you some good."

The Darley stood still while Clint put the saddle on him and cinched it into place. As Clint walked him outside, he noticed the big horse was not limping. He hoped he would remain that way.

He looked over at the house, waved to Zelda, who was on the porch with her rifle. He mounted up and headed for the Wheeler ranch.

***

Hattie Wheeler was sitting on the porch of her house, waiting for Dave and Leonard to return with whatever help they had gone to fetch. She thought about the time she had spent on her kitchen table with Clint Adams when they first met, and was sorry that he was going to have to die. But she had very little choice. And with a little luck, he'd kill her two step-sons at the same time.

The Salish, Ben, watched the Wheeler house from hiding, seeing only Hattie Wheeler at that moment. He had arrived before daylight, and hid in the hayloft of the barn. He had not yet seen any sign of Kent Wheeler, or the sons, Dave and Leonard. He figured the woman was waiting on the porch for the boys or the husband to return.

Then, since she was on the porch, he decided to circle around to the back of the house and try to get a look inside. Maybe he could learn something helpful to tell Clint Adams when he arrived.

***

Clint was happy with the way Eclipse made the ride. The horse was frisky and had to be held back from galloping. That was a good sign.

When he came within sight of the Wheeler ranch he reined in and watched it for a short time He didn't spot any sign of the three Wheeler men. At one point, though, he saw Hattie Wheeler come out onto the front porch and sit. She was waiting, but for what and who?

And where the hell was Ben?

Chapter Thirty-Nine

Clint decided to leave Eclipse far enough away from the ranch as to go unseen, but not so far that he would have to walk a mile. He made his way to the barn and went inside. For a working ranch, he was surprised to find no horses in the corral, and none inside.

"Ben," he whispered. "Ben, are you in here?"

No answer.

He studied the dirt floor and saw the prints of a naked foot. Could've been Ben's tracks. He was anxious to move, but he decided to give it a few more minutes.

It took only five for Ben to appear.

"There you are," Clint said, as the Salish entered. "You've got to be more careful, it could've been somebody other than me, in here."

"I knew you were here," Ben said.

"So where were you?"

"I hid in the loft, but then I went to the house to look inside."

"Did you get in?"

"No," Ben said, "but I looked in the window."

"And?"

"I saw blood."

"Where?"

"On the floor, in the kitchen."

"Is Hattie still on the porch?"

"Yes."

"And no one else is around?"

"No."

Clint thought a moment,

"I'm going to go and talk to her," he said, finally.

"Is that wise?"

"Right now it's just her," Clint said. "Maybe I can get something out of her. But first I've got to get my horse."

"You rode Eclipse here?"

"I had no choice," Clint said. "I'm not as spry as you, I couldn't walk here."

"I have seen only seventy suns," Ben said.

"That may be," Clint said, "but you've got to be more careful." He pointed to the ground. "You left tracks."

The Salish was staring downward as Clint left to go and fetch Eclipse.

***

Clint mounted Eclipse and rode him to the house. He gave Hattie credit, when she saw him she didn't even flinch. Just remained seated and waited.

"Mr. Adams," she said, as he reached the house. "What brings you here? And with your wonderful horse."

He dismounted and put one foot up on her porch.

"I thought it was time we talk," he said.

She was wearing a simple cotton dress, but it was designed to cling to her curves. She probably put them on display for "her boys."

"So," she said, leaning forward so that the neck of her dress gaped, "talk."

"Why don't we go inside?"

She sat back.

"No, we can talk here."

"Hattie, I want to know who's behind your offers to buy Zelda's place."

"What makes you think somebody's behind it?" she asked.

"Because your husband's not smart enough."

"For what?"

"Well . . . anything, really."

She stared at him, then started to laugh.

"Oh," she said, getting her breath back, "I needed that. You know, you're totally right about him. And his sons are just as stupid."

"Then what's a smart woman like you doing here?" Clint asked.

"You think I'm smart?" she asked. "I ain't got much of an education."

"I think you're . . . crafty," he said. "Tricky. Smart doesn't mean you have to be educated."

"You're educated, ain't you?"

"I have some education, yes," Clint said. "From back East. Ages ago."

"But you came west and became a legend."

"That's what they tell me."

"Well, I came west to try to get rich," she said.

"With Kent Wheeler?"

"He told me he had a big ranch," she said.

"And kids who needed a mother?"

"I didn't find that out until I got here," she said, "and by then we was already married."

"I take it back," he said. "Maybe you aren't smart."

"Or," she said, leaning forward again and wetting her lips, "maybe I wasn't, but I am now."

"Well, Hattie," Clint said, "I've got another question for you."

"Yeah?"

"Yeah," he said. "Whose blood is on your kitchen floor?"

Chapter Forty

"What?"

"There's blood on the floor in your kitchen," Clint said. "If you were cleaning it up, you didn't do such a good job."

"How do you—" She looked past him, saw the Salish step out of the barn and start toward them. "Oh, your trained savage?"

"He's got a keen eye," Clint said. "Who got killed in your kitchen?"

"What makes you think somebody got killed?"

"I'm guessing it was Kent."

"Why would I kill my husband?"

"Because he was going to keep you from getting rich," Clint guessed. "Did he know who gave you the money?"

"No."

"But he was doing what you told him?"

"Yeah," she said, "until you got to him. Then last night, he tried to get rough. He'd done it before, but this time I didn't put up with it."

"So you killed him."

She nodded.

Ben reached them. Clint looked at him.

"The two boys are coming," he said, "and they have help."

Clint turned back to Hattie.

"And now the boys are gonna kill you."

***

This time Hattie had no choice.

Clint grabbed her am, pulled her out of her chair and dragged her into the house, with Ben right behind.

"How many riders?" Clint asked.

"Seven," Ben said. "Maybe eight."

Clint looked at Hattie.

"You sent them for help?"

"I told them to do whatever was necessary to get the job done," she told him.

"And the job was to kill me?"

She shrugged.

"Sorry."

"I'm sure you are."

"No," she said, "I really am. I enjoyed our time together, Clint. I thought . . . maybe . . . we might get to do it again, some time."

"But I guess that's not going to happen, is it?"

She looked surprised.

"You would be willing?"

"I'd prefer it to having to kill those two young men," Clint said. "Do they even know you killed their father?"

"No," she said, "and they're not gonna."

"How do you expect to keep them from finding out?" She smiled.

"They're gonna think you did it."

"Where's his body, Hattie?"

She didn't answer.

"Ben," he said, "find something to tie her up with."

Ben nodded. He went through the house quickly, came back with some rope. They tied her hands and feet, then Clint paused before gagging her.

"You'll regret all of this," he told her, "when your whole family is dead."

"They were never my family," she said.

He gagged her.

Ben was looking out the window.

"They are coming."

"You stay inside," Clint said. "At the window. I want them to think I'm alone."

"Why?"

"It's the advantage I'll have," Clint said. "And you have to make every shot count."

"I always do," Ben said.

Clint nodded, and stepped outside.

As Dave and Leonard rode toward the house they saw the front door open, and a man step out.

"Is that your father?" one of the men with them asked.

"No," Dave said.

"Who is it?"

Dave squinted.

"Jesus," he said, "that's the Gunsmith."

The man smiled. His name was Tony Gaines, and he was the first one the boys had gone to. He then collected the other men, promising them a chance at the Gunsmith.

"Well, that's who we're here for, ain't it?" he asked.

"Yeah, right," Dave said.

"Dave?" Leonard said, riding up alongside his brother.

"This is it, Lenny," Dave said. "This is what Hattie wants us to do."

"What about Pa?"

"Hattie's gonna have to take care of Pa," Dave said. "Right now, we gotta take care of the Gunsmith. Okay?"

"Yeah," Leonard said. "Okay."

Gaines came up alongside them.

"This is what we're gonna do . . ." he began.

Chapter Forty-One

Clint watched as the men approached, but suddenly two veered off to the right, and two to the left. He backed up to the window.

"They're splitting up," he called out to Ben. "You better go to a back window."

"Are you sure?"

"Go!"

Ben left the front window, ran across the house to the back.

Clint stood waiting for the riders who were still coming straight for him—four of them. He could see two of them were the Wheeler boys.

***

"Slow down!" Gaines called out.

The four men—Dave, Leonard, Gaines and a man named Larkin—slowed their horses to a trot.

"He's waitin' for us," Leonard said.

Gaines looked at him. He was in his thirties and considered himself an expert with a gun. Dave and Leonard knew Gaines and his friends stayed at an abandoned line shack on the Wheeler ranch when they were trying to avoid the law. They had offered them a lot of money, and a chance at the Gunsmith.

The Wheeler boys were about to cash in on one of those things.

***

Clint watched as the men slowed. They were giving the others time to get into position. The only chance Clint had to avoid gunplay was to convince the Wheelers that Hattie had killed their father. Maybe then, they'd turn on her.

He could have taken some shots as they approached, but he waited.

***

"Gaines," Leonard called. "Shouldn't we start shootin' at him?"

"No," Gaines said, "he ain't shootin'. Let's get closer."

"Ain't you afraid of him?" Leonard asked.

"No," Gaines said. "It ain't his time, anymore. It's mine! Just a little closer."

***

Clint stood with his rifle in his left hand, and his right hand hanging down by his Peacemaker. Hopefully, they would want to talk, too.

First…

***

The four men reined in their horses in front of the house, about twenty feet from Clint.

"You're Adams?" Gaines asked.

"That's right," Clint said. "And you?"

"Gaines," the older man said, "Tony Gaines."

"Never heard of you," Clint said.

"Not many have," Gaines said, "but after today they will."

"You think so?"

"I know so."

Clint looked at the two Wheeler boys.

***

Ben watched from the back window as two men approached the house on horseback. He couldn't see any others. They were probably coming from a different direction.

He did the only thing he could think of—broke the window, stuck the barrel of his rifle out, and fired . . .

***

"You boys should know your father's dead," Clint said.

"You killed him?" Leonard demanded, his face turning red.

"No," he said, "Hattie did."

"You're a liar!" Dave blurted.

"She must've told you she was going to take care of him," Clint guessed. "What did you think she meant?"

Before the boys could decide, they heard shots from behind the house.

And all hell broke loose . . .

***

As the four men drew their guns to start firing, Clint drew faster, and made sure that nobody would ever know who Tony Gaines was by shooting him first. Gaines went over backwards, off his horse and fell to the ground.

The others began firing and Clint dove off the porch to find cover, aware that there was still shooting coming from the back of the house. He was going to have to depend on Ben to handle it, while he handled the front.

The three shooters were not only shooting, but fighting for control of their horses. Clint hated to do it, but he shot the horse that Leonard was on. It went over on its side, pinning the boy beneath its weight, and he screamed out in pain.

The others immediately leaped from their horses.

***

Behind the house Ben fired again at the approaching riders. He knew he had hit one, but the man kept coming. The other man's horse stumbled at the last minute, causing Ben's shot to miss. He fired two more times in quick succession. He knew he would have been more accurate with a bow-and-arrow.

And where were the other two men?

***

Clint watched the two men hit the ground and scramble for cover, only there was none. He realized they were the Wheeler boys.

"No place to go!" he shouted. "It's over."

Both Wheelers got to their feet and started to look around for a place to hide. That's when there were shots from Clint's left.

Clint turned, saw the other two men coming at him on foot. As he turned to address them, he realized there were no more shots from the back of the house. And then Ben came out the front door, with his rifle in front of him.

"Watch out!" Clint shouted, as Ben stepped right between him and the approaching shooters.

The old Salish immediately dropped to his knees and turned. Clint then left those two shooters to Ben, and turned back to the Wheelers.

Both young men were confused. One was down on one knee, wild-eyed, desperately searching for something—cover, help. Anything.

The other—he thought it was Dave, the older one—dropped down onto his belly, but he was as pop-eyed as his brother. They were both in a situation that was beyond them.

Ben sent two shots toward the approaching shooters and, unlike with the two in the back, he didn't miss.

Then he turned to the two brothers and levered another round.

"Wait!" Clint shouted.

Ben looked at him.

"Don't shoot."

The Wheeler boys were still looking for a way out.

"Drop your guns, boys," Clint called. "You've got no cover, and no chance."

Glassy-eyed, they stared at Clint and Ben.

"Dave?" Leonard said.

"Drop your gun, Lenny," Dave said. "It's over."

Gratefully, Leonard dropped his gun.

Chapter Forty-Two

Dave got to his knees, and then to his feet, but he still held his gun.

"You, too, Dave," Clint called out to him. "Drop your gun, boy."

"Were you tellin' the truth?" Dave asked. "Hattie killed our Pa?"

"Yes," Clint said, "she did."

Dave tossed his gun away.

"Where is she?"

"Inside."

"Where's he?" Leonard asked.

"Also inside." Clint pushed the barrel of Ben's rifle down so that it was pointing at the ground. "Come on in."

Both boys walked towards the house. Clint let them go in first. They stood looking at Hattie Wheeler, tied and gagged on the floor.

"Where is he?" Dave asked.

Clint and Ben came in behind them.

"I'm going to guess this house has a root cellar?" Clint said.

"Yeah," Dave said, "it does."

Hattie's eyes went to a point on the kitchen floor. Clint followed her glance, and saw the outline of a door.

Dave started for the door.

"Why don't you let me?" Clint asked.

"No," Dave said. "He's our Pa."

Leonard rushed to help his brother lift the door. They didn't have to go much further. Hattie had simply rolled him over and dumped him down the stairs. He was lying at the bottom, his chest matted with blood, the ground around him soaked.

Leonard looked at Hattie.

"Now why'd you go and do a thing like that?" he asked.

***

They lifted Hattie Wheeler onto a chair. She remained tied and gagged.

Clint allowed the boys to go outside and round up the bodies.

"Their guns are out there," Ben reminded him.

"They won't try to pull anything," Clint said. "They're done."

"So what do we do now?" the Salish asked.

"I'm not sure," Clint said. "There's no law near here."

"We could leave her to them," Ben said. "She killed their father."

Clint looked at Hattie. Her dress was slightly askew, revealing some of the skin of her breasts.

"I don't know," Clint said. "She killed their father."

Ben looked at her, said, "But she could still have some power over them."

Clint went to her and straightened her dress, making it less revealing. She glared at him defiantly.

"I don't think so," he said. "They seemed pretty upset about their dad. Maybe we should just leave her to their justice. I think, after they bury their father, they wouldn't want to keep her around very much longer."

Her eyes flared. She didn't like that idea.

"But before we do that . . ." Clint said, pulling the gag down from her mouth.

"You can't do that," she said. "They'll kill me."

"You think so?"

"I think I could convince one of them not to," she admitted. "but not both. Just let me go. I'll leave and never come back."

At that point both boys came back inside. They glared at Hattie. Clint saw that they had not retrieved their guns.

"What do you say, boys?" Clint said. "She says she'll leave and never return. You want to let her go?"

"No!" Leonard said. "She killed Pa!"

Dave was a little calmer.

"We talked about it outside," he said. "We're sorry, Mr. Adams." Suddenly very respectful. "We shouldn'ta never come after you, or Miss Zelda. It was all her idea."

"Everythin' was her idea!" Leonard barked. "We never shoulda listened. And now Pa's dead."

"And the money she and your pa were offering to buy Zelda out?" Clint said. "Do you boys have any idea where that came from?"

"No idea a-tall, Mr. Adams," Dave said. "They never told us."

"I don't think your pa ever knew," Clint said. "I think only she did."

Clint looked at Hattie.

"Where's the money?"

"It ain't here," she told him. "We never got it, yet. Once Zelda agreed to the price, I was supposed to go and fetch it."

"Well then," Clint said, "that brings up the next question, don't it?"

The two boys stared at him, confused. Ben looked at him, and nodded. Even the old Salish knew what he was getting at, now.

"What about it, Hattie?" Clint said to the bound woman. "You think you want to tell us where that money was going to come from?"

Chapter Forty-Three

Clint rode back to Zelda's while Ben walked alongside.

"You can ride up ahead," the Salish said. "I will be there."

"There's no hurry," Clint said. "I just hope we made the right decision."

"They will kill her," Ben said. "I looked into their eyes. I think you were right. She will not be able to control them both."

"That's what I meant," Clint said. "I hope we made the right decision leaving them."

"She killed her husband," Ben said, "and she told them to kill you."

"I remember, Ben," Clint said. "I remember."

They traveled the rest of the way in silence.

***

When they reached the ranch, Ben took Eclipse into the barn to unsaddle and rub down. Clint went to the house. Before he got there, the door opened and Zelda came out. She remained on the porch, and when he stepped up she threw her arms around him and hugged him tightly.

"Worried?" he asked.

"Not at all," she said. "Is it over?"

"Yes."

She looked past him.

"Is Ben all right?"

"Yes, he's in the barn with Eclipse."

"What happened?"

"Let's go inside and I'll tell you."

***

Zelda listened intently without asking any questions until he was finished.

"So Kent is dead?"

"Yes."

"And you believe the boys will kill Hattie?"

"Yes."

"They're not killers, Clint."

"They were going to kill me," he reminded her.

"In a gun battle, with the help of others," she said. "What makes you think they'll kill a woman?"

"Because the woman is Hattie, and she killed their father," Clint said. "You didn't see their eyes, Zelda."

"Well," she said, "I suppose whether they kill her or not, it's all over."

"Maybe."

"What else can we do?"

"There's one thing," he said, "but I'll do it when I leave here."

"And when is that gonna be?"

"Tomorrow morning," Clint said.

"That soon?"

"It's time," Clint said.

She reached across the table to touch his hand.

"Yes," she said, "I suppose it is. What about Ben?"

"He might stay around a bit longer," Clint said, "if you ask him."

"I never had much of a father," she said. "And I ain't had a ranch hand in ages."

"He could probably fill the bill on both counts," Clint said.

"I'll have to ask him, then," Zelda said.

"You can do it at supper tonight," he said. "Uh, there is going to be supper tonight, right?"

"Oh yes," she said, "I'm gonna give you quite a send-off, and supper is only part of it."

Chapter Forty-Four

Clint said goodbye to Zelda and Ben—who had decided to stay for a while longer—and rode away on Eclipse, who felt very solid beneath him. He had both of those people to thank for that, and for his own return to health, as well.

From Zelda's ranch he rode directly to the small no-town of Halsey, where he reined in Eclipse in front of the trading post and went inside.

"You're back," Farley said, from behind the counter.

"Ah, you remember me," Clint said.

"Hard to forget the man who saved my business, and probably my life. Beer?"

"Sure."

"Where ya headed?" the man asked, setting the luke-warm beer down in front of Clint.

"Just away," Clint said. "Away from here, on to somewhere else."

"Just driftin', huh?"

"Pretty much."

"I ain't never had that kinda life," Farley said. "I wonder how I woulda done."

"Well," Clint said, "you're doing pretty well for yourself here, aren't you?"

"Yeah, sure," Farley said, spreading his arms. "Look what I got."

"Oh, you've got more than this place, don't you, Farley?" Clint asked.

"Whataya mean?"

"Well," Clint said, "you had the money to buy the Wheeler place, and you're trying to buy Zelda Carter's ranch."

"Wha—who told you all that?"

"Who do you think?"

"Well, I dunno," Farley said, "because none of it's true. Zelda Carter's a good customer of mine."

"According to Hattie Wheeler," Clint said, "you're trying to buy up as much land around here as possible. Seems you think this area's going to come to life soon, and you want to be a big part of that."

"And where would I get the money to do all that?" Farley asked.

"That she didn't know," Clint said. "Maybe you could tell me."

"Nowhere, that's where," Farley said. "This is all a bunch of crap."

"I don't think so," Clint said. "You see, I believe her."

"No," Farley said, "I mean, it's a bunch of crap that she told you all that. She wouldn't."

Clint frowned, pushed the lukewarm beer away.

"This is funny," Clint said.

"What is?"

"You haven't asked me where Hattie is," Clint said, "or how she is. Why is that?"

"If she's passin' lies about me," Farley asked, "why would I care."

"No," Clint said, straightening up and looking around. "There's something else going on here."

"Like what?"

"You didn't ask me about her because you know where she is," Clint said.

Farley didn't respond.

"Damn it!" Clint swore.

He was convinced now that he had been wrong to leave her with the Wheeler boys. After everything she'd done, including killing their father, she had still been able to control them after he and Ben left.

"They're here, aren't they?" Clint asked. "They got here before me, and told you what happened. Don't touch that shotgun!"

Farley froze.

Chapter Forty-Five

"Back up," Clint said.

Farley stepped back until he bumped into the shelves behind him.

"You make a move and I'll put a bullet in you."

Clint reached over, found the shotgun and brought it out. It was an over-and-under Greener.

"Where are they waiting?" he asked. "Outside? In the back?"

Farley didn't answer.

"No, not out back," Clint said. "Outside, across the street. Waiting for me to come out so they can bushwhack me?"

"Look," Farley said, "she's a strong bitch—"

"Oh, don't tell me, she's given you a poke or two? Got you to do what she wants?"

"Adams, there could be a lot of money involved, here." Farley said. "Why don't you just—"

"Why don't you just shut up and lie down on the floor behind the bar," Clint said. "Go ahead, do it. And don't get up until I tell you to."

"But I—"

"If I see you before then, I'll assume you have a gun and I'll kill you."

Farley immediately dropped to the floor behind the counter.

"Good man," Clint said.

He walked to the front window, still holding the shotgun, but that wouldn't do him any good if they remained across the street. And his rifle was outside, on his saddle. He was going to have to rely on his Peacemaker.

But that was all right, because it had never let him down, before.

***

"Should we go in after him?" Leonard asked Hattie.

"No," she told him, "just stay where you are and keep your rifles ready."

They were in an abandoned building across the street, at the windows which had no glass in them.

"This better work," Dave said. "When he finds out we didn't kill you—"

"And why would you kill me?" she asked, putting her hand on his back and rubbing it. "Don't I give you boys what you want? Plus, there's going to be money in this for all of us."

"If everything develops the way Farley says it will," Dave pointed out.

"Just shut up and be ready," Hattie said. "Adams is comin' out any minute."

***

"Is there another way out of here?" Clint asked Farley.

"No back door, if that's what you want."

"How about a window?"

"In the back, yeah," Farley said.

"Okay," Clint said, "lead the way."

Farley walked to a door in the back with Clint and into his storage room. In the back wall were two windows.

"Okay," Clint said, "tied up, or a bump on the head? Your choice."

"Oh, well, tied up, I guess."

"Too bad." Clint hit him over the head with a nearby axe handle. "Tying you would take too long."

He dropped the handle and went to the window, opened it and climbed out.

He was able to easily circle all the way round to the back of the building across the street. It was the only place that made sense.

Like the trading post, there was no back door. But there was a window. He didn't even have to open it, though, because there was no glass. He climbed into the back room, and heard voices from the front.

He moved to the doorway and peered in. There was a man at each of the windows, and behind them a woman he recognized, even from the back.

"Okay," he said, stepping in, "everybody just stand still."

The two men tensed.

The woman turned, despite Clint's order, and smiled.

"Clint," she said, "how nice."

"Hattie," he said, "I'm actually glad to see that you're not dead."

"The boys, they just couldn't do it. Could you boys?"

"Uh, no, Hattie," Dave said, and Leonard just nodded.

"But you boys are holding rifles," Clint said. "That means you were ready to kill me when I stepped out of the trading post."

"Can you blame us?" she asked. "You just about ruined everything. But I knew you'd be coming here to see Mr. Farley, after I gave you his name."

"But you were serious," he said. "He is the one with the money."

"Yes," she said, "but not the brains."

"No, that's you," Clint said. "Use your brains now, Hattie. You and the boys should leave."

"We can't do that, Clint," she said. "But you could use your brains, and join us. Then you and me, we could—"

"Hey!" Dave said, half turning, "you said you and me—"

"Shut up, Dave!" she snapped.

"I won't!" Dave said, turned quickly, bringing the rifle around.

"Dave!" Leonard yelled, also turning.

Clint knew he had no choice, this time. He drew and fired twice, and each man was driven through their window by the impact of the bullet.

Hattie turned, saw the boys go through the windows, their rifles dropping at her feet.

"Don't, Hattie," Clint said.

She looked at him.

"Only one way you're gonna stop me, Mr. Gunsmith," she said, with a smile.

She leaned over slowly, grabbed one of the rifles, and straightened.

"Aren't you gonna kill me?" she asked.

"Why?" he asked. "You've got no more help. You're alone, Hattie."

"But I have the Wheeler ranch, and soon I'll have the Carter ranch."

"You have to leave Zelda alone, Hattie."

"I can't do that, Clint," she said. "Sorry, but I have to kill her."

"You're not giving me a choice," he said, holstering his gun.

"No, I'm not," she said, "because I'd rather be dead than livin' the way I've been livin'."

"Hattie—"

"Sorry," she said, and turned toward him with the rifle.

He had to put an end to it all and keep Zelda safe. As he drew, fired and watched his bullet punch into her chest, he could only remind himself that this was a vile, hateful woman.

Coming March 27, 2019

THE GUNSMITH
445
The Curse of the Gold City

**For more information
visit:** www.SpeakingVolumes.us

On Sale Now!

THE GUNSMITH
443

For more information
visit: www.SpeakingVolumes.us

On Sale Now!

THE GUNSMITH *series*
Books 430 – 442

For more information
visit:

Coming Spring 2019

Lady Gunsmith 7
Roxy Doyle and the James Boys

For more information
visit: www.SpeakingVolumes.us

On Sale Now!

Lady Gunsmith 6
Roxy Doyle and
the Desperate Housewife

**For more information
visit:** www.SpeakingVolumes.us

On Sale Now!

Lady Gunsmith *series*
Books 1-5

For more information
visit:

On Sale Now!

ANGEL EYES *series*
by Award-Winning Author
Robert J. Randisi (J.R. Roberts)

**For more information
visit:**

On Sale Now!

TRACKER *series*
by Award-Winning Author
Robert J. Randisi (J.R. Roberts)

On Sale Now!

MOUNTAIN JACK PIKE *series*
by Award-Winning Author
Robert J. Randisi (J.R. Roberts)

CPSIA information can be obtained
at www.ICGtesting.com
Printed in the USA
LVHW030001140220
646864LV00003B/402

9 781628 159882